THE boyfriend WHISPERER 2.0

LINDA BUDZINSKI

Swoon
ROMANCE

THE BOYFRIEND WHISPERER 2.0 by Linda Budzinski
All rights reserved. Published in the United States of America by Swoon Romance. Swoon Romance and its related logo are registered trademarks of Georgia McBride Media Group, LLC. No part of this book may be used or reproduced in any manner whatsoever without written permission of the publisher, except in the case of brief quotations embodied in critical articles and reviews.

Trade Paperback ISBN: 978-1-948671-67-5
ePub ISBN: 978-1-948671-74-3
Mobi ISBN: 978-1-948671-75-0

Published by Swoon Romance, Raleigh, NC 27609
Cover design by Danielle Doolittle

To Deb, Karen, and Ted

THE boyfriend WHISPERER 2.0

Chapter
ONE

I sink back into the booth and rub my temples. I'm not sure whether this headache is from my mango smoothie or because my ex just strolled into the Juice Joint with his arm around Becca Marsh.

My two best friends, Maggs and Brie, shoot me a look.

"What is this, his third girlfriend since you two broke up?" Brie curls her lip. She's never been a Ty Walker fan. "That boy has commitment issues."

Maggs points her straw at me. "His problem is, you've ruined him. He can't find anyone else who measures up to the fabulous Alicea Springer."

I smile in spite of the pickaxe to my cranium. "Yeah. I'm sure that's it."

Ty is everything I could ever want in a boyfriend: athletic, super cute, and really, really, *really* smart. He's this season's leading scorer for the Grand View High School soccer team, and he's applying to go to Harvard, Princeton, and Penn. He's the perfect guy for me. Well, except for the whole dumping-me-a-week-before-junior-prom thing.

Not that I'm bitter. Now that we're almost two months into our senior year, I'm ready to move forward, with or without him. Preferably with.

"Someday soon, he'll realize we're meant for each other," I say, eyeing his calves, so tanned and muscular and perfectly Ty. "He'll come crawling back."

"That I'd like to see," Brie says. "Actual crawling. And maybe some bawling."

Our chatter stops as Ty and Becca pass our booth on their way toward the back of the restaurant. Becca shoots me a sly smile, while Ty completely avoids eye contact.

"Did you see that? He never even glanced at me as he walked by." I try to sound casual, but my voice catches. And Maggs, of course, catches the catch.

She takes a sip of her ginger-mint tea and leans forward. "Know what? He's not worth your time. You deserve better."

"Agreed," Brie says. "Way better."

"And you'll get it." Maggs's tone is serious. "I know you will. The universe has a way of working these things out."

I force a smile. That's easy for them to say. No guy has ever broken Maggs's heart. She's always the one to break up with them. And Brie has been dating Blake Myers since sophomore year. He's at UVA now, but they're so in love, they're even making the long-distance thing work. Neither of them quite understands what I went through last year to get Ty to notice me and what it was like to lose him.

"I don't want better." I say. "I want Ty. He's The One. We belong together."

Brie sighs. "Do you really believe that?"

"I do."

She and Maggs exchange glances. "Well, we know how you can convince him." Brie wiggles her eyebrows at me, and I can see exactly where she's going.

"Sorry. Not happening. We've been through this a million times."

"Come on, Alicea. Boy-friend Whis-per-er." She teases out each syllable. "Libby has brought together so many happy couples. Why not at least try her?"

Libby is the matchmaking computer program I developed this summer, after I became president of Boyfriend Whisperer Enterprises. Her name is short for LIBACA, which is short for Love is But a Click Away.

My predecessor, Lexi Malloy, started Boyfriend Whisperer Enterprises last year to help the girls at our high school snag their crushes. She was a modern-day Cyrano de Bergerac, spying on her targets and anonymously coaching each client on how to get her crush's attention.

Lexi's model was very successful … until it wasn't. Turns out telling guys exactly what they want to hear isn't the path to true love. Most of her couples—and her business—fell apart toward the end of our junior year.

That's when I offered to take over and give the business an upgrade—one that uses actual data and formulas to pair up couples. It took me all summer to perfect my program, but Libby is easy to use and super accurate. My clients log in, take the survey, and find their top Grand View High match.

My only role is to collect their money and keep my mouth shut.

"I have no intention of using Libby," I assure Brie. "I already found my perfect match."

"But if Ty is——"

"He is," I say. "And I don't need Libby to tell me that."

"Of course you don't." Maggs reaches across the booth and grabs my hand. "But maybe it would help for her to tell *him*."

I narrow my eyes at them. "Why are you two teaming up on me?"

"What?" Maggs's eyes widen. "This isn't about teaming up."

"Come on, Alicea," Brie says. "You know Libby works. What are you afraid of?"

"I'm not afraid."

"But——"

"But nothing. This conversation is over." I nod toward the restrooms. "Be right back."

I head into the ladies' room, where I slump against the sink, tears threatening. The fact is, Brie's right. I am afraid. Afraid Libby would pair me up with someone other than Ty. Any other guy at Grand View would be a step down—a major step down. If I can't have him, I don't want to date anyone.

I lean forward and study myself in the mirror. We came straight from our Tuesday afternoon ballet class, so my hair is twisted into a bun. I let it down and shake it out. The girl staring back at me is pretty. Not beautiful, but certainly pretty. She's smart and has a good sense of humor and is even a fairly talented dancer. Yet she's not good enough for Ty. Not perfect enough for him.

The sound of a bolt opening in one of the stalls startles me. I'd thought I was alone. I grab a paper towel and wipe at the smear of mascara below my eye.

"Well, hello, Alicea." Becca appears beside me, studying me in the mirror. "Nice leotard. So you're still dancing, even after … ?" Her voice trails off, and she smirks.

My face burns. She doesn't have to finish. I know exactly what she's talking about—junior prom. I may or may not have made a complete fool of myself on the dance floor after the infamous dumping. Will I ever live that night down?

"Yep." I force a smile. "Still dancing."

"And whispering?"

"And whispering."

"How's that going?" Her tone oozes skepticism.

"Awesome. As of this morning, I had almost two hundred clients."

"Really?" She takes a lipstick out of her pocket and carefully applies it. "So who are some of the couples you've matched up?"

"You know I can't tell you that." I get asked this a lot, or people ask who so-and-so's match is, but I keep Libby's results confidential. "I can tell you that there are almost two dozen Boyfriend Whisperer couples who are dating right now."

Becca smacks her lips and turns to look me in the eye. "Interesting. And yet you remain single and alone."

I'm tempted to snap—to tell her my perfect match is the boy she walked in here with—but instead, I shrug. "I'm not in the game right now. I have other priorities."

"Of course you do." Her smile hovers somewhere between condescending and cruel. "Like maybe inventing another program? How about one that magically makes losers less ... loser-y?"

I scowl as she turns on her stilettos and struts out the door. I haven't thought of myself as a loser in a long time. Not since I hired Lexi to help me catch Ty's attention almost a year ago.

Wow. It feels like another lifetime. I turn to my reflection and remind myself of the advice Lexi gave me in that first email, the one that changed everything.

You're beautiful and brilliant, and you have a voice that matters. Now use it!

I'd read the email over and over for weeks before I believed it. Of course, I didn't know it was from Lexi at the time; she kept her true identity a secret. I just knew it was from the Boyfriend Whisperer. It had been a bold move, hiring her to set me up with the most sought-after guy at Grand View High. In fact, I puked immediately after submitting my application. But her success rate was phenomenal, and my crush on Ty knew no bounds. I'd risk anything to get him. I followed every step of every set of her instructions. I switched desks in civics partway through the second quarter so I could sit next to him. I just "happened" to drive up one day after soccer practice when he had a flat tire to offer him a ride home. I even created a mini video for him starring an animated hero that looked and sounded a lot like him.

Finally, after a few weeks, Ty asked me out. I found myself in a different world, going to all the best parties, cheering for Ty at his soccer games, and riding around Sterling in the front seat of his silver BMW coupe with the windows down and Bruno Mars blaring on his sound system. I "came out of my shell," as my mom liked to say, and even made friends with two girls from my dance class whom I had always found a bit intimidating but who turned out to be the best things to ever happen to me—Maggs and Brie.

Yes, dating Ty was the best four and a half months of my life. Until the dumping.

My stomach still clenches when I think about it. A bunch of us had gone to Laser Nation. Ty and I were on the yellow team. We stuck together, but partway through our third round, we lost each other. As I crouched behind a barrier wall trying to figure out my strategy, Chris Broder appeared around the corner wearing a vest for the blue team. I have horrible aim, but Chris is our basketball team's star center. He's huge and would have been impossible to miss, so I shot him square in the chest.

"Nice hit," he said.

I flashed a smile and rushed by him before he could recover. "Have you seen Ty?"

Chris pointed to the far side of the room. "I think he's over by red team's home base."

I wove my way through the maze of barriers and pillars, getting shot a half dozen times as I went. I had a bad feeling about this. Ty had been acting strangely all night long. All week, if I was being honest. He was moody and quiet, and our kiss when he picked me up tonight had been all lips and no heart. Something was wrong. I knew it.

My sense of dread grew as I neared my destination. As I turned the last corner, two red guards zapped me. I ignored their whooping and chest bumping and pushed past them into the base. And there I found ... nothing.

"Hey, you."

I swiveled at the sound of Ty's voice. He'd come in behind me.

"I've been searching all over for you."

"You have? I mean, me too. I've been looking for you." I pulled him out of the base and into a dark corner, but when I tried to kiss him, he pulled away. The feeling of dread welled up again in my chest, my lungs, my throat. "Ty? What's wrong?"

He sighed and looked away. "I think we should take a break."

"A break?"

"Yeah. Not necessarily forever, but ... you know." His eyes met mine. "For now."

My heart pounded in my ears. For now? As in, a week before prom? People do not break up the week before prom, especially when they've been nominated for king and queen. Even a one-time social misfit like me knew that. Unless ... "Who is it?"

Ty shook his head. "There's no one else. Listen, I'm sorry. You're an amazing girl, and the past few months—"

"Five. Almost."

"Five. Right. They've been great, but, I mean, come on. We both knew this wouldn't last forever."

Did we? I couldn't count the number of times I'd daydreamed about visiting Ty at college, spending spring breaks together at the beach, and making plans for our future. My dreams usually ended with him getting down on one knee.

"Of course we knew," I lied. "But prom is next week. If you want to take a break, why not wait until after?" Even as I said it, I knew it sounded stupid and lame and desperate and whiny and, well, basically all the things I actually felt at that moment.

Now, six months—and, as Brie so kindly pointed out, three girlfriends—later, we're still on "break." I know I should forget about Ty. Move on to bigger and better things, as Maggs says. Problem is, there is no one better as far as I'm concerned.

"Alicea? Are you okay?" Brie appears in the bathroom doorway. "Your smoothie's melting."

"I'm good." I offer a bright smile, though I have no doubt Brie can see through it.

She joins me at the mirror and drapes her arm around my shoulder.

"What does he see in Becca?" My voice cracks, and I glance away from our reflections. One of the faucets is dripping, and I have an urge to smack it. "She's kind of a wench."

"I saw her strut out of here. Did she say something to you?"

"No. I mean, she asked some questions about the whispering, but ... " I leave off the part where she basically called me a loser. "It's her attitude, you know? She's not right for him. He deserves someone better."

"Like you?"

"Precisely."

"Then prove it." Brie holds up her phone and taps it, pulling up the Boyfriend Whisperer app. "Come on, Alicea. What do you have to lose?"

I bite my lip. Maybe Brie is right. Sure, part of me is terrified that Libby won't match me with Ty, but what if she does? We were so perfect together. No doubt she'll get it right, and at last I'll have proof that we belong together. Sitting around waiting for him to figure it out himself clearly isn't working.

I sigh and grab Brie's phone. "Nothing. Nothing to lose at all."

Chapter THREE

Libby asks sixty-four questions, all designed to figure out my clients' likes, dislikes, and personality traits, as well as their beliefs about some of the Big Questions in life. Since I created it and have had lots of time to think about my answers, I tear through it. Maggs and Brie sit on the edges of their seats watching as I click through, screen by screen.

Finally, I reach the last question.

LIBBY Question #64: Which of the following would be part of your ideal vacation?
A. Surf
B. Snow
C. Ruins
D. Tents

I tap "Surf." My finger hovers over the bright pink "Love Is But a Click Away!" button as my heart pounds and my headache returns.

"Go on. Do it." Brie's eyes shine as brightly as though she's about to find her own true love.

I tap the button. The screen fades to gray as Libby goes to work, matching me with the boy of my dreams. Meaning, with Ty. It has to be. I hand the phone to Brie. "Here. I can't look. Tell me what it says." I turn to glance at Ty and Becca laughing and holding hands in their booth. "No, wait. Don't tell me unless it's him." I squeeze my eyes shut and wait.

After an interminable amount of time, Brie emits the faintest of grunts. "Huh."

My eyes fly open. *Huh?* What does that mean? Brie is frowning. Crap. Or … not crap? Brie doesn't like Ty. Maybe she's upset because it's him. I sit frozen to my seat, unsure whether I want to know.

Brie shows Maggs the phone, and her eyes widen. "Oh, my."

Oh, my. That can't be good. I grab for the phone, but Brie pulls it away. "Maybe this wasn't such a great idea."

I hold out my hand. "Give it. Now." My heart is racing, and I fear I might puke up my smoothie. Whose name is on that screen?

Maggs snatches the phone and sets it face down on the table. "Forget it. Libby screwed up."

I glare at them both. Maggs has always been skeptical of my whispering model, but I know better. Libby doesn't screw up. I reach over and wrest the phone from her grip.

```
Darius  Groves.  Certainty:  97%  -  A  Near
Perfect Match!
```

No.
Wait. Make that Nooooooo. Capital N, capital Ooooooo.

Chapter FOUR

Darius Groves is not Ty. In fact, Darius Groves is the anti-Ty.

"This can't be. It's not possible." I shake my head.

Maggs and Brie eye me warily.

"Are you okay?" Maggs asks.

I hold up Brie's phone and glare. "I'm awesome. Why wouldn't I be? I've just been matched with a criminal."

Brie rolls her eyes. "He's not a criminal."

"Practically a criminal. A deadbeat, for sure."

"Come on. You barely know him. He might be a nice guy."

"Right. Because nice guys get expelled from school all the time."

Darius transferred to Grand View at the beginning of this year. Rumor has it he was kicked out of his old school for fighting. He's not stupid—he's in my advanced English lit and calculus classes—but he sits in the back row and zones out and occasionally makes stupid cracks that send all the cretins in the room into hysterics and land him in detention.

"You know, looks-wise, he's kind of cute," Maggs says.

"Don't even."

"No, I mean it. You should see him in his gym shorts." She nudges Brie. "He's ripped."

"Ah, yes, gym." I lean forward. "Aren't you the one who told me he pulled a guy's shorts down on the track a couple of weeks ago? Who does that?"

"Oh, please." Maggs offers a nervous smile. "It was no big deal. He was messing around. I don't think he actually meant to—"

"Hey, Alicea."

We all startle at the sound of Ty's voice.

I slap Brie's phone face down onto the table and press my hand firmly on top of it as though it might flip itself over. "Hi, Ty." My voice comes out as a squeak.

Becca lingers beside him, a possessive pinkie curled around a belt loop in his shorts.

"You must have just come from dance," he says, taking in our leotards. "How's that going?"

"Good. It's … super fun." *Brilliant, Alicea.*

"Alicea is leading the corps in the dance we're learning," Brie says.

"Yes. She's fantastic. So graceful." Maggs smiles sweetly.

"That's cool. Maybe I'll check out your next recital." With that, Ty circles an arm around Becca's waist, says goodbye, and ambles out the door. The familiar scent of his cologne lingers behind, and I catch my breath. How was I not matched with him?

I offer Maggs and Brie a smile. "Thanks for bragging on me, you guys. I appreciate it."

Brie shrugs. "It's what friends do."

"I meant every word," Maggs adds.

"So what do you think about that?"

Brie squints. "About what?"

"The fact that he made a point to say hi. And invited himself to our next recital."

"Well … " Maggs hesitates. "I think he was being … nice."

"Yes, nice. He was being nice. Don't turn it into something it's not."

I stick out my tongue. "It's not as though I think we're going to get back together again tomorrow, but you have to admit, it's a step. After all, he didn't have to say he'd come to the recital. He volunteered that."

"He said 'maybe.'" Brie points out. "And by 'maybe,' he meant 'probably not.'"

Maggs jabs Brie with her elbow. "Actually, I hope he does show up so he can see what he's missing. Because you, Alicea Springer, are a much better catch than Becca Marsh."

I smile, though I know Maggs is just being kind. Becca is model-thin, flirty, and can pull off wearing stilettos at the Juice Joint, while I am … none of that. I close my eyes and conjure up Lexi Malloy's email. *Beautiful and brilliant.* That's easier to believe some days than others. Some days I feel as though Ty and I belong together forever, while others, I barely feel as though I'm good enough for—

"Ack. I gotta roll."

I slide Brie's phone across the table to her, jump up, and rush toward the exit. I need to get home to my computer and delete my survey before Darius logs on and finds out we've been matched.

That is, if it's not already too late.

Chapter FIVE

Ms. Arken hands me a stack of calc problems. "Pop quiz. Pass these down your row."

A chorus of groans rises up as I take one and twist to hand the rest to the girl behind me. As I turn back around, my eyes meet Darius's. I glance away, probably too quickly. *Was he staring?*

I swear Darius smiled at me as I walked into class today. In the short time since he started at Grand View, I have rarely seen him smile. He must know. And of course, he knows I know. This is a disaster. My breathing grows shallow, and the problems on the sheet in front of me blur into a mass of incoherent numbers and symbols. A bead of sweat forms at the nape of my neck and trickles down my back.

"Darius, is there a problem?" Ms. Arken's voice interrupts my mini-meltdown.

I risk a glance back to find Darius slumped at his desk, the only person not tackling his quiz.

"Dropped my pencil," he says, pointing in my direction.

I look down to find that, sure enough, his pencil is beside my desk. Ms. Arken levels a skeptical stare at him, and then at me. My cheeks burn. No way did a dropped pencil travel the length of six desks and three rows. He had to have rolled it here on purpose.

I reach down, pick it up, and hold it out, but Darius makes no move to come get it. His mouth twists into a half-smile, and he folds his arms across his chest. I have the urge to throw the pencil at his head, but instead, I hand it to the girl behind me. "Can you pass this back?"

I try to return my attention to my quiz, but my brain is jumbled, and when Ms. Arken calls time, I still have three questions unanswered. Ugh. As everyone passes their papers back up the row, I feel a tap on my arm.

"Psst. Alicea. I need to talk to you." Aiden Jackson leans across the aisle toward me, a pleading expression in his eyes. "Think we can meet up for a few minutes after school?"

I frown. I barely know Aiden. He's on Ty's soccer team, but we've never hung out. "Meet up about what?"

He glances around to make sure no one else is listening. "My match. I need your help."

"Sorry." I shake my head. "Not happening."

"Please?" He sits up straight as Ms. Arken passes by. When the coast is clear, he leans over again. "You're the Boyfriend Whisperer. You have to help me."

I shake my head. "I don't. That's not how whispering works anymore."

"What do you mean that's not how it works? What did I pay you for?"

I glare. "You paid to take the survey and find your match. After that, you're on your own. I stay out of it."

"But—"

Ms. Arken clears her throat and throws Aiden a death-stare, shutting him down. Thank goodness. I steal another glance back at Darius. I have enough problems dealing with my own supposed match. The last thing I need is to get tangled up in someone else's.

Maggs, Brie, and I have lunch together on B Days. So does Ty. I love B days. Or did. Turns out Becca is also in our lunch period. I'd never noticed before, but now that she's clinging to Ty like ivy to the towers of Princeton, it's impossible not to. I clutch my tray of chicken nuggets and march past them.

"He knows," I announce as I set down my tray and slide into my seat.

"Who knows?" Maggs asks.

"Knows what?" Brie adds.

"Darius Groves. He knows."

"What?" Brie's eyes widen. "Why do you say that? Did you mention something to him?"

"Of course not, but I can tell." I share the saga of the

"dropped" pencil. "Plus, he keeps staring. And smiling. And possibly winking." I note their skeptical expressions. "I'm serious. I think he winked at me as we walked out of calc."

"I don't know about the winking," Maggs says, "but the staring I can believe. Because, look at you, girl. Is that a new eye shadow?"

I smile. I did wear a new shade today, a smoky gray that brings out the blue in my eyes. Ty always said he loved the color of my eyes, and I was planning to talk to him this afternoon about next week's recital. I even brought a flyer to give him, if only he weren't so … wrapped up.

I lean in toward Maggs and Brie and lower my voice. "The sooner I can get back together with Ty, the sooner my Darius Groves problem disappears. That's my priority."

Brie groans.

I turn to her. "I know Ty's not your favorite, but—"

"It's not just that."

I purse my lips. "Then what?"

She pauses, as though choosing her words carefully. "You're always saying Ty is so perfect, and maybe he is, but that doesn't mean he's perfect for *you*. And then Libby finds *your* match, using an algorithm *you* created, and you call him a 'problem.' I don't get it."

"Brie." Maggs's tone is soft.

"I'm just saying that maybe you should reconsider. Besides, have you noticed the full-court PDA happening over at Ty's table?" Brie points her carrot stick at me. "You're the one who insists Libby never makes mistakes."

I open my mouth to argue, but nothing comes out. I grab my tray. "You know what? I'm not hungry. I think I'll go to the library and do some studying."

"Alicea." Maggs gives me her puppy-dog eyes. "Don't be like that. You know Brie is trying to—"

"I know. I'm not being like anything. I just need to brush up on my French vocab." I hurry away, dumping my nuggets in the trash on my way out the door. As soon as I hit the hallway, I take off and run toward the nearest girls' restroom, where I proceed to wipe off every trace of my stupid smoky-gray eye shadow.

I'm mad at Brie for thinking I don't deserve Ty and belong with someone like Darius. I'm mad at Maggs for taking Brie's side. I'm mad at Becca for hanging all over Ty, and I'm mad at Ty for letting her. But most of all, I'm mad at Libby. How could my own program betray me like this?

Chapter
SIX

Later that afternoon, Aiden grabs my arm as I'm about to board my bus. "Five minutes. Please?'

I pull away. It's chilly, and I'm wearing a too-light sweater. I can feel the heat emanating from the bus door, and I want nothing more than to get on, sit down, and bury my head in a game on my phone. "I told you. I can't help you."

"But—"

"But nothing." The dejection on Aiden's face makes me feel bad. Almost. "Who is it, anyway? Your match?"

"I'm not telling you. Not if you're not going to help me."

I refrain from reminding him that if I truly cared, I could go home and look it up in my database. I sigh. "Aiden, this person is your match. Libby says so, and Libby is never … I mean, she's … " I turn away. "You have nothing to worry about. Go for it. It's meant to be."

I hurry onto the bus and slip into my usual seat in the third row on the right side. I used to believe it when I told people their match was meant to be. Now, I'm not so sure.

Ms. DuBois resembles a tiny, furious bull as her foot stomp-stomp-stomps against the dance floor. She has a right to be angry. This rehearsal has been a disaster, mostly because of me. I've screwed up half a dozen times in the first twenty minutes.

I take a deep breath, assume second position, and prepare to perform our *demi-demi-grand plié* combination. I step into an *en pointe* and twirl to the left and … slam into Hannah.

"Hey!" She tumbles backward into Jalika, who falls into Maggs in a mini human-domino display. "What the heck?" Hannah rubs her shoulder.

"Ladies, ladies. Enough." Ms. DuBois glares at me, and I can practically see the steam curling from her nostrils. "Alicea, what is the problem? It is as though your head is in the clouds while your feet are stuck in cement."

My face burns, but I say nothing. It's a fair critique.

"Into my office." Ms. DuBois points and instructs the other girls to run through the combination on their own.

I scurry in and park myself on a bench against the wall, eyes on my feet, braced for the lightning storm to come. Ms.

DuBois rarely gets angry, but when she does, it's scorched earth.

"Life Saver?"

I peer up to find her holding out a roll of the fruit candies, her eyes showing no hint of the rage that flashed moments ago. I take one and pop it into my mouth, uncertain whether to trust this sweet gesture. "Thank you."

She takes a seat behind her desk and regards me for a long minute over her glasses. "I've seen significant improvement in your technique over the past few months. As well as your positioning."

"Thank you. I've worked hard."

"I know, and that is why I chose you to lead the corps for this dance. But today ... you are not yourself. What is the problem?"

"Nothing. It's ... I've been distracted. I'm sorry. It won't happen again."

"What is distracting you?"

I shrug. "Personal stuff." No way am I telling Ms. DuBois about Ty and Becca and Darius, no matter how gentle her tone or how many Life Savers she plies me with.

She sighs. "We all have personal stuff, Alicea. We need to—"

"I know. Put it aside. I will, I promise."

"That is not what I was going to say." She stands and comes around the desk toward me. "Dance requires us to give of our whole selves, and that 'personal stuff' is part of who we are. Do you understand?"

I nod, though I have no idea what she's talking about. We just saw what happens when I bring my baggage to the dance floor, and it's not pretty.

"You need to let it in. All of it. Make space for the personal stuff, and let it work for you."

I nod again and add a small smile for good measure.

She sighs and claps her hands. "Chin up. You turned the wrong way, but your technique was perfect. Until you collided with Hannah."

That elicits a real smile. Ms. DuBois rarely jokes. It's always good to see her sense of humor. I stand to go. "Thanks. And I'll think about what you said."

She reaches up to brush a stray tendril of hair from my face. "Trust yourself more, Alicea. Not only your mind, but your instincts, your gut, and your heart. Trust, and make them work for you."

As we emerge from her office, twelve sets of eyes turn to stare. Maggs mouths, *You okay?*

I nod as I take my spot in the center of the line. I am okay. In fact, I'm more than okay. Ms. DuBois is right. I need to trust my heart and my mind and make them work for me.

My heart is telling me I should be with Ty and should do whatever it takes to get him back.

And my mind just realized how I can make that happen.

Chapter SEVEN

I close my eyes and hit PRINT. My stomach rolls in rhythm with the laser jet. I swore I'd never do this, but then again, I never dreamed I'd be matched with Darius Groves while watching Ty fall for Becca. Desperate times call for desperate measures.

When I first launched Libby, I sent her to some of the most popular kids in class for free. I figured that would bring in clients who hoped to get matched with them. I hated to include Ty, but since I'd sent the survey to most of his teammates, I kind of had to. I worried he'd find a match with someone other than me, but to my relief, he hasn't. His highest match to date is sixty-two percent, and it's with Brie, who doesn't like him, already has a boyfriend, and would never even have taken the survey if I hadn't asked her to beta-test the mobile version for me.

One thing I promised my clients was that I would never read their responses. In fact, their answers were encrypted so that I couldn't. But today in dance class, with Ms. DuBois urging me to use my heart and my mind, it occurred to me that since I wrote the code, I could also rewrite it.

"Yo, Geekazoid."

My brother's voice startles me. I jump up and grab the pages off the printer.

His eyebrows shoot up. "What's that?"

"Nothing." I sit down and flip them over in my lap.

Andrew thinks Boyfriend Whisperer Enterprises is silly. Of course, he's making nine dollars an hour mopping floors at Italiano's to put himself through college while my job at this point mostly entails logging into my account to see how much money has been deposited. And it's usually a nice sum.

He steps toward me, still eyeing the sheets in my lap. "What are you up to?"

"Nothing. Go away. And maybe try knocking next time?"

"Fine." Andrew grins, backtracks, and knocks on my already opened door. "Yo, Geekazoid. Mom just called. She and Dad have a meeting tonight at the gallery, so we're on our own for dinner." He rests his hand on the doorknob but makes no move to leave.

"And?"

"And … there's some leftover chicken in the fridge, but I thought maybe we could order a pizza."

"Sure. Whatever." *Now leave me alone.*

"The thing is … "

I roll my eyes. I know exactly what the thing is. "Seriously?"

"It's not that much. Italiano's is having a half-price special."

"Then why can't you afford it?" I reach over, open my desk drawer, and grab a ten. "I know, I know. Poor college student." I hand him the money. "Here. Anything but anchovies."

Andrew smiles, grabs the bill, and heads out with a mumbled, "Thank you."

I sigh in relief and carefully turn over the pages on my lap. A combination of dread, guilt, and excitement rushes through me. I've always stayed out of this end of the business, not only to protect my clients' privacy but also because I have no desire to meddle in their love lives. Is this how Lexi felt when she was the Boyfriend Whisperer? Did her stomach knot up when she staked out her targets?

I take a deep breath and read through Ty's survey answers. Most are exactly what I would expect. I know he's ambitious, thinks zombies are greater than vampires, and loves sports and Italian food. But some of his answers surprise me. Would he really pick fame over true love? And is it true he thinks it's more important to be right than to be fair?

I go through and highlight the responses that seem most useful—the ones I can capitalize on for Mission Win Back Ty. I know what I'm doing is wrong in so many ways, but at the end of the day, gathering this intel on him is not that different from what Lexi did for me last year. It worked then, and it could work now. It has to.

Chapter
EIGHT

"I want you to have fun with this," Mr. Dunham says in English class the next day. "Be creative."

I steal a glance at Ty, already calculating how I can make sure we end up as partners. Our teacher wants us to recreate scenes from classic literature as modern-day retellings. It's the perfect opportunity for the two of us to spend some quality time together.

Mr. Dunham takes off his glasses and wipes the lenses with the bottom of his sweater. "I had planned to let you choose your own scenes and partners, but I think it'll be easier if I assign them," he says.

What? No. I scan the room and quickly do the math. I have a 4.2 percent chance of being paired with Ty. The odds are definitely *not* in my favor. Then I spot Abi Eisenberg with her hand raised.

"Mr. Dunham?"

"Yes, Abigail?"

"What if we already know what we want to do?"

Yay, Abi.

Mr. Dunham perches his glasses at the tip of his nose and peers over them. "What did you have in mind?"

Abi grins. "Roland and I would like to do a scene from *Cyrano.*"

That elicits a round of laughter. Abi was Lexi's assistant last year at Boyfriend Whisperer Enterprises. It's a perfect choice for her and her boyfriend.

Mr. Dunham nods and makes a note on his tablet. "That's fine. Anyone else?"

I take a deep breath and raise my hand.

"Alicea?"

I glance at Ty, who has his phone on his lap and appears to be surreptitiously texting someone. I bite my lip. "I was thinking maybe *Romeo and Juliet?* The balcony scene?"

Mr. Dunham nods. "Lots of potential there. Do you already have a partner lined up?"

I turn again toward Ty. He looks up from his phone, but I can tell by his expression he hasn't heard a word of the conversation. Still, I summon up my courage and ask, "What do you think, Ty? *Romeo and Juliet.* You in?"

He turns to his right and his left, searching the faces of our classmates for an answer, a lifeline, or a clue as to what's happening. Everyone is watching him expectantly, and a few kids are snickering.

"Um. No?"

The entire class bursts out laughing.

"Ouch."

"Shut down."

"Awkward."

I turn to face the front of the room, training my eyes on the whiteboard. My face is on fire, and the air has become thick and heavy.

Mr. Dunham quiets the room. "Enough, enough. Alicea, do you want to ask someone else, or should I assign a Romeo?"

I don't trust my voice, so I simply shake my head.

"Does that mean, no, you don't want to ask someone else, or no, you don't want me to—"

"I'll do it." A voice from the back of the room pipes up.

Oh. My. Gosh. The class falls silent, and everyone turns to stare. Everyone but me. My eyes never leave the board.

"Darius?" Mr. Dunham sounds as shocked as I am. Though not as mortified.

"Yeah. I'll be Alicea's Romeo."

My classmates' laughter has been replaced with stunned gasps and murmurs. If our teachers gave out participation trophies, Darius wouldn't even be in the running. What possessed him to speak up? Of course, I know. It's Libby's fault.

"Very well." Mr. Dunham points his stylus at me. "Alicea, does that work for you?"

I nod. "Sure." It comes out part whisper, part croak.

The rest of the class slips by in a blur as everyone gets paired up for scenes. Mr. Dunham tells us we have three weeks to prepare our retelling, and he wants us to perform it in front of the class. *Awesome.* When the bell rings, I dash out the door, but Ty calls after me.

"Alicea."

I pretend not to hear him.

"Alicea, hold up."

I stop just outside the door and lean against the wall, my eyes on the ceiling to stave off the tears lurking just below the surface.

"I'm sorry. I didn't know what was going on. You shouldn't have sprung that on me."

"Really?" I take a chance and meet his gaze. "If you had known, would you have ... never mind. It doesn't matter." I hate the desperate edge in my voice, and I hate how much it does matter. I hate how the simple act of standing here next to him sends my heart racing. I want to reach out, grab his hand, and saunter down the hall with him like last year. I want to once again be the girl lucky enough to date Ty Walker.

"Wherefore art thou?" Mickey Adams croons with a mocking falsetto as he exits the room and passes us, sending two girls behind him into a fit of giggles. Ty punches Mickey's arm, but he's laughing, too.

I straighten and turn to go. "It's no biggie. In fact, I'm sure Darius will do a great job and we'll ace the project. That was my main concern." I force a smile, offer what I hope is a breezy wave, and take off down the hallway.

Darius Groves. My Romeo. Can someone please just poison me now?

Chapter
NINE

The grays, blacks, and purples slam together to form a cloud that matches my mood. Below the painting, a plaque reveals its title and price: *Scattered Seashells – $250*. The scattered part I can see. The seashells, not so much. And 250 dollars? Um. No. I wouldn't pay twenty-five cents for it.

Tonight I am neither the Boyfriend Whisperer, nor the smartest kid in my programming class, nor the girl who can't seem to get it together at dance. Tonight I am merely a body.

My dad manages the Loudoun Art Gallery, and my mom teaches classes here. The gallery sits two floors above Ms. DuBois's studio, in the county arts center. Each month, Mom holds an exhibition for her students. Unless we have a good excuse, Andrew and I are expected to show up—to be warm bodies and to feign interest in the artwork. At least, I feign interest. Andrew actually inherited my parents' love of art, and their talent for it as well.

"'Scattered Seashells.' Very cool." Andrew saunters up to me holding a heaping plate of cheese and crackers. "Reminds me of de Kooning."

I swipe a slice of cheddar, roll my eyes, and mutter, "Reminds me of something I drew when I was five."

"There you are!" My mother barrels down the hallway, arms open for a hug. "Thank you for coming." She lowers her voice. "We really needed you two tonight. Must be the rain keeping people away, but these folks have worked so hard. I hope we can make a few sales."

She plants a kiss on each of our foreheads before turning and whirling away to greet more guests.

I turn back toward the painting. "They've worked so hard? How hard can it be to slap a bunch of random splotches on a canvas?"

Andrew snorts and launches into a lecture on contrasts and perspective and a bunch of pretentious art terms I don't understand and have zilcho interest in. I gaze at the painting and pretend to listen while helping myself to more cheese and plotting my next move with Ty.

```
LIBBY Question #33: Which of the following
is your favorite holiday?
A. Christmas
B. July 4
C. Halloween
D. Thanksgiving
```

According to his survey, Ty loves Halloween best, which is perfect, as the holiday happens to be two weeks away.

Everyone knows he loves all things *Star Wars*, so a Princess Leia costume might be just the thing to catch his attention. Besides, I've always wanted to do that bun thing with my—

"Hey, Alicea! Can we talk?"

I turn to find Aiden Jackson once again walking toward me. Oh, jeez. What's he doing here?

"I'm, uh, kind of busy," I say.

His gaze falls on the painting. "Is that a de Kooning?" he asks my brother.

What the—? I've never even heard the word "Dekooning" before. Or is it two words? "No, it's a nobody," I say. "Some student."

"Well, I'm somebody, though certainly not de Kooning." A grandmotherly woman appears beside us. "But I'll take that as a huge compliment."

"I'm so sorry," I say. "I wasn't … I only meant … "

She laughs. "No need to apologize. I know what you meant." She raises her eyebrows at me as though she understands exactly what I think of her painting before turning toward the boys. "Do you think two-fifty is too much to ask? It seems pricey. Then again, did you hear what the latest de Kooning went for at auction?" She glances around, and when none of us answers, she practically shouts, "Sixty-six million! Broke a record."

I choke on a cracker. Sixty-six million? Dollars? For something that looks like a kindergarten project gone awry. *What is wrong with people?* As the woman begins discussing her technique, I try to slip away and leave the three de Loonies to their art talk. Unfortunately, Aiden notices and chases after me. "Yo. Hold up."

I sigh and wait for him. "The answer is still no. I can't

help you."

My mother waves to me from across the room, a huge grin on her face. At least I might score some points for bringing in another body.

"Please?" Aiden grabs my arm. "I'm begging you."

Something about the desperation in his voice tugs at me. I motion for him to follow me over to the drinks table. All that cheese has made me thirsty, and I pour us each a glass of punch. "Helping people hook up is not part of the deal, you know. I make the match. That's it. I honestly don't know if I can—"

"You can. I'm sure you can. And if you do, I'll owe you. I'll help you with … whatever you want."

I sip at my soda and consider this. Aiden and Ty aren't great friends, but they do hang with the same soccer crowd. "What about Halloween?" I ask.

"What about it?"

"Do you know of any parties? Any that your teammates might be going to?"

Aiden nods. "Yeah, sure. Baldwin's having something next Saturday."

I smile. Jack Baldwin and Ty hang out a lot. He'll definitely be there. "Can you get me an invite?"

"Are you offering to help with my match?"

I squeeze my eyes shut and nod. "I'll do what I can."

"Cool. Then I'll get you an invite."

"Awesome. So, who is it? Who's your match?"

Aiden's shoulders sag ever so slightly. "It's Maggie."

"Maggs?"

"Maggs."

"Oh, my." *You poor, poor boy.*

Chapter
TEN

Maggs's full name is Sugar Magnolia Blossoms Blooming Maloney. Her parents were total hippies when they had her, though now they're as straight and narrow as two people can get.

Unfortunately for them, Maggs takes after their younger selves. A free spirit who answers to no one and constantly flakes out, Maggs frankly would drive me up a wall, except that she also is one of the kindest, sweetest human beings I've ever known.

Well, except when it comes to guys.

It's not that she's mean to them. She's not. In fact, she's pure Sugar, and she combines that sweetness with a *c'est la vie* attitude that drives boys crazy and keeps them coming back for more. Until she very sweetly breaks their hearts. Which she does. Every. Single. Time.

"I'm in way over my head." I pick up a duster and fluff its feathers against my palm. Lexi Malloy, Abi Eisenberg, and I are standing in the F Hall janitor's closet. The two of them used to meet here in secret back when Lexi was the Boyfriend Whisperer and Abi was her assistant. There's no reason for us to hide now, since my identity isn't a secret, but when I texted and asked to see them, Lexi suggested we come here for old times' sake. "I've never actually set anyone up, much less Maggs," I tell them. "Can you help me?"

Lexi shakes her head. "Sorry, chica. I'm out of the whispering business. You're on your own."

I look at Abi, but she raises her hands in protest. "No way."

"Why did you agree to help Aiden, anyway?" Lexi asks. "You've always insisted that's not how you roll."

I shrug as I pluck a feather out of the duster. I have no intention of telling them about the Halloween party and Ty and my not-quite-fleshed-out plan to get him back. "Because I'm an idiot, that's why." I snap the feather in two. "What am I going to do?"

Lexi snatches the duster from me. "You're going to stop destroying school property, for one. And you're going to make good on your promise. That's what Boyfriend Whisperers do. No matter how stupid and misguided and doomed to failure our promises may be."

Abi shoots Lexi a side-eye. "Is that your idea of a pep talk? Because if it is, I think you've lost your touch."

Lexi laughs and threatens to puff Abi in the face with the duster, but Abi swats it away. "Shouldn't Maggs know about the match by now?" Abi asks. "It would show up when she logs onto the app, right?"

I nod. "Except she never logs on. She only took the survey as a favor for me. Maggs doesn't believe in Libby. I think her exact quote was, 'Love isn't about algorithms. It's about destiny.'"

"So that's it." Abi points her finger in the air as though she has discovered the most obvious and simple solution in the world. "You need to convince her that Aiden Jackson is her destiny."

Lexi and I both stare at her.

"Okay. And how do I do that?"

Abi shrugs. "No idea. You can't expect me to have *all* the answers."

The fourth-period warning bell rings, and Abi opens the closet door. "Gotta run. Good talk, girls. And Alicea, you've got this. You're pretty much the smartest student at Grand View, and you know Maggs better than anyone. If you can create a computer program like Libby, you can problem-solve this."

I can't help but smile. "You think so?"

"I do."

"Thanks. That means a lot."

"Sure thing." Abi turns to Lexi, eyebrows raised. "And that's how pep talks are done."

Lexi threatens Abi again with the duster, sending her shrieking into the hallway. Lexi pauses and hands it back to me before heading out herself. She gives me a quick hug. "Abi's right, you know. If anyone can pull this off, you can. I mean that."

I lean against the closet door and watch them both

disappear down the hallway and around the corner. I hope they're right.

The bell rings again, meaning I'm late for my fourth-period study hall. I close my eyes and groan. I almost forgot, or maybe I was subconsciously blocking it from my mind. Darius and I agreed to meet this period to begin planning our balcony scene.

Darius Groves. My supposed match. How do I problem-solve *that*?

Chapter
ELEVEN

I find Darius in the back corner of our study hall lounge at an otherwise empty set of carrels, his head buried in a giant volume of *The Complete Annotated Works of Shakespeare*.

"Sorry I'm late."

"No problem." He raises his head slowly, deliberately, and gives me the once-over. He offers a half-smile and points to the book. "I have an idea for our retelling."

Oh, dear. I'd assumed the one advantage of working with Darius would be that he would have no ideas. "Well, that's wonderful," I say as I sit down beside him. "But I already have everything worked out. I know exactly how we'll play this."

"Is that so?" Darius's eyes widen in what I think is amusement, and he pushes his too-long curls off his face. "Do tell, oh bright angel. Or in a modern day retelling, I guess that would be more like, 'Talk to me, hottie.'"

I glare and force myself to ignore the fact that Darius Groves has just called me hot. "Texts," I say.

"Texts?"

"Yep. We pull off the entire scene as a series of texts up on the screen. What could be more modern than that?" *And what better way to avoid standing in front of the whole class, including Ty Walker, to declare my love for a total loser?* "So instead of me saying, 'Parting is such sweet sorrow,' I'll text, 'Gotta run before my parents catch me. ttyl.' Or maybe 'c u later.' You know, with the 'c' and the 'u.'" I draw the letters in the air.

Darius nods. "Mmhmm. And I assume that would be followed by a frown emoji?" He draws one of those in the air.

I start to answer, then realize he's making fun of me. Seriously? Mr. Pull-Down-a-Kid's-Shorts-in-the-Middle-of-Gym-Class has the nerve to mock my brilliant idea?

"Emojis happen to be a very popular form of modern communication," I say. I hate the fact that I sound so defensive and like such a … geekazoid. "Personally, I think it's a great idea. It'll be funny, and if we do a good job with it, we can pull an 'A.'"

Darius's eyes meet mine. His head is tilted slightly, his expression contemplative. When he speaks, his tone is soft. "Please tell me you can see the difference between 'Parting is such sweet sorrow' and a frown emoji."

I look away, flustered by his gaze. "Of course I can see the difference. But I'm not Shakespeare, and neither are you, and people don't talk like that anymore. They do things like send frown emojis."

Darius sighs, and his shoulders sag.

"Fine," I say. "Let's hear your idea."

He shifts in his seat and eyes me warily, as though he's no longer sure he can trust me with it. "Romeo and Juliet were from rival families, right? That's why they couldn't hook up. So how does that translate today? In high school?"

I screw up my lips as I consider this. "Gangs? Like the Jets and the Sharks? 'Cuz that's already been done."

Darius shakes his head.

"Ah, so you want to go the jocks-versus-nerds route. Also been done."

His expression deflates and I feel kind of bad for being a jerk, even though he made fun of my idea first.

"It doesn't have to be jocks and nerds." He leans toward me. "It could be anything. Take your pick. How about … " He snaps his fingers. "The prom queen and the class troublemaker?"

It takes a moment for his words to register, but when they do, I can feel the heat rising on my cheeks. Darius must have heard that Ty and I were up for prom king and queen last year. Does that mean he also knows Ty dumped me right before prom, and what a fool I made of myself?

Darius leans back, picks up a pen, and twirls it in and out among the fingers of his right hand. "Imagine that Boyfriend Whisperer program of yours. What if the prom queen got matched up with somebody she'd never in a million years dream of dating? What then?"

Get out. Did he seriously go there? I turn away so he can't see the panic that must surely be registering in my eyes. *Pull it together, Alicea. Pretend you have no idea what he's talking about. If you don't admit to the match, it's as though it never happened.* I take a deep breath and turn back to him. "You know what? Fine. We can do the prom queen and the troublemaker, but we're doing it with texts. Deal?"

He smiles and holds out his hand to shake. "Deal."

Chapter
TWELVE

One ... two ... three. One, two, three. One, two, three. I sit cross-legged on the floor of the dance studio, eyes closed, reviewing the dance over and over in my mind. The sequence hasn't made its way into my muscle memory yet, and I can't afford to have another practice like last week.

"Hey, Alicea. Can you help me?" Maggs interrupts my mental rehearsal. She sits across from me, legs splayed, trying to stretch out her limbs. Scattered throughout the room are girls stretching and doing barre exercises and warm-up routines.

I get up and walk behind her to press her lower back with my palm, easing her forward.

"Perfect," she says, her voice slightly strained. "Now, can you stay there forever so I can hold this position?"

"Sure. How about a massage while I'm at it?"

"Oooh, that sounds amazing. Do you have any hot stones on you?"

I laugh and glance at the clock. Five minutes until rehearsal starts. "So, um. I've been meaning to ask you. Jack Baldwin is having something at his house Saturday. For Halloween."

"Mmhm." I feel Maggs tense ever so slightly under my fingertips. She knows Jack and Ty are friends. She probably already sees where this is going. Or, at least, partly where it's going.

"Anyway, we're invited, and it's been a while since I've been to a good party, and—"

"Alicea." Maggs stops me. "I get it. You're invited, Ty's going to be there, and you want to go. End of story. Amiright?"

"I guess." *Except for the end-of-story part.* Maggs would almost certainly rebel against a computerized Libby set-up, so that plot twist will have to remain a secret. "So, will you go? It'll be fun."

"Of course I will. What kind of friend would I be if I said no?"

"Cool." I breathe a small sigh of relief.

Maggs nods toward Brie, who is over by the mirror practicing her *arabesque* position. "Did you ask her?"

I nod. "Yes, but she and Blake have a horror movie marathon planned." I try to sound as though I'm disappointed, but in reality, I'm relieved. The last thing I need is Brie judging me all night. "So, anyway. What do you think you'll dress up as?"

Maggs shrugs. "I have to think about it. What about you?"

"I'm thinking Princess Leia." I try to assume a casual tone, but it doesn't fool Maggs.

She twists her head around to give me an eye roll. "Shocker."

My cheeks grow warm. I hate that I'm so obvious, so predictable.

Her tone softens. "Actually, I think that's a great idea. You'll be the most adorable Leia ever."

"Thanks. Also, I may need your help with the sticky-bun thingies."

"No problem." Maggs slides her hands out along the floor, and I press down, extending her stretch another couple of inches. "Maybe I'll go as a hippie," she says.

I laugh. "You can probably pull that off." Maggs owns more boho shirts than anyone I know, and her basement is filled with bins of her mom's old bleach-ripped jeans, beads, and crystals. "So by 'maybe,' do you mean 'maybe,' or do you mean you'll definitely go as a hippie?"

Maggs twists her head around again. "Why do you care?"

I shrug and look away. "No reason. Just curious."

But Maggs doesn't have a chance to answer, because at that moment, Ms. DuBois bursts into the room, clapping her hands and shouting. "Let's go, ladies. We're going to start with a walkthrough today. I don't want any more mishaps or missed turns."

She doesn't look directly at me, but we all know who she's referring to.

I take a deep breath and assume my position, front and center of the corps. *Come on, Alicea. You've worked too hard for the past five years to screw up now, especially when Ty might come to the recital.*

I close my eyes and lift to *en pointe. Let's do this.*

Chapter THIRTEEN

When I was twelve, my parents decided I needed to cut down on my screen time. They insisted I take up two new activities—one artistic and one physical. I can barely draw a stick figure and am horrible at any sport involving balls, so my options were limited. I briefly tried the oboe and track, but I spent so much time at lessons and practices that I got my first-ever "B" on a report card.

Then, one day, they dragged Andrew and me to an exhibit at the National Gallery of Art. I lingered in the Impressionist section, where the paintings at least resemble the things they're supposed to depict. I happened upon Renoir's "The Dancer," and it hit me. The dance studio below the gallery: two birds, one stone.

To my surprise, I was good at it. Not a natural, certainly, but someone who, with a lot of hard work and practice, could eventually master a *foette*.

I still don't particularly understand art, but I do now have a soft spot for Renoir, which is why I'm standing in the Loudoun Art Gallery gift shop Thursday evening admiring a nine-by-twelve print of "Luncheon of the Boating Party" when I hear the door open and a familiar voice.

"Alicea?"

I freeze. Darius Groves. What the—is he stalking me?

I turn to find him in the doorway of the shop, his hair wet from rain, his long-sleeved gray t-shirt clinging to his chest. I try to ignore Maggs's voice in my head pointing out how ripped he is.

"Fancy meeting you here." I grit my teeth, partly because that makes it sound as though I would want to meet him somewhere, and partly because it is perhaps one of the geekiest things to ever come out of my mouth.

Darius nods toward the print in my hand and walks over. "That's one of my favorites. Those people were Renoir's friends. See this guy here?" Darius stands so close I swear I can feel the steam coming off him. "That's Gustave Caillebotte. The painter."

I nod. "Interesting." I start to shove the print back into its bin, but Darius catches my wrist. "And this woman. The one with the little dog? Renoir eventually married her."

Inexplicably, the fact that Darius Groves is semi-holding my hand while talking about marriage sends my heart racing. I pull my hand from his and angle my body away, steadying myself against the counter.

"There you are, sweetheart. Did you bring my phone?" My mother bursts into the room, stopping as she notices Darius. "Do you two know each other?"

Darius turns to me, his eyes wide. "Ms. Crofton is your mom?"

I get that a lot since my mom kept her maiden name. "Yeah, I ... " I what? *I assumed you knew that this was my parents' gallery, and that's why you came here in the pouring rain in the hopes of finding me?* Kind of makes me sound like an egomaniac.

"Yep. She is. This is her phone. She forgot it." I hold it out as though it's some sort of genetic ID. "Wait. How do you know her?"

"Darius is one of my most promising new students," Mom answers for him. She walks over and drapes an arm around his shoulder. "A real talent, this one."

I glance back and forth between them. "Talented? At art?"

Darius tilts his head, a half-smile playing on his lips. "Why is that so hard to believe?"

"Because ... I don't know. It's not. It's ... whatever." What can I say? *Because I hate art and you're supposed to be my match?*

"You're getting a private lesson today," Mom says to Darius. "Some sort of flu going around. The other three students in the class called in sick."

"Oh, well, if you want to cancel until next week—"

"No, no." Mom smiles. "You're here. Class is on. That is, if you don't mind being the only one."

"No, of course not." Darius turns to me. "Unless ... do you want to sit in with us?"

I blink and force a smile. Darius Groves. Art class. Am I being punked? I refuse to look at my mom, because I know all too well the hopeful glint that must be shining in her eyes at the thought of her daughter taking one of her classes. "I don't think so. I—"

"Come on," he says. "It's mixed media. It'll be fun."

I hesitate. I am curious to see how much artistic talent someone who is supposed to be my match could possibly have. Besides, it would give me a chance to run some of my ideas for our balcony scene by him.

"It's settled, then." Mom snatches her phone from my hand. "I knew there had to be a reason I forgot this. It's fate."

Fate? *Lovely*. Now both Libby and the Universe are conspiring against me.

Chapter **FOURTEEN**

"It doesn't have to be perfect." Darius grins as he watches me slice away at a magazine headline, forming the shape of a flower petal.

"That's right," Mom chimes in. "Art is not about perfection. Often it is about appreciating the imperfect."

I force a smile. I was strictly a color-inside-the-lines type of kid, while Andrew would scribble and scrawl and splatter all over the place. My parents always hung both of our projects on the fridge, but I could tell they gravitated toward his brand of "art." It never made sense. How can you break all the rules and still be good?

I hold up my petal in defiance. It is in fact perfect, and I managed to clip it so that the word "bloom" appears directly in the center where I wanted it. It is my seventh perfect petal, and I place it in the last remaining spot on my flower.

As I apply an acrylic matte to seal everything into place,

Darius strolls over to my easel and inspects my work. He reads the petals clockwise from the top. "Sun. Air. Rain. Soil. Sprout. Reach. Bloom." He nods. "I like it."

I frown and point to the "Reach" petal. "I couldn't find 'Grow' in a font I liked," I say. "Can you believe that? I must have gone through four magazines, including one all about gardening. Maybe I should have kept searching."

"No, no." Darius shakes his head. "Don't you see? 'Reach' is better. It's the twist that makes me want to root for your flower. No pun intended."

I groan, but I can't help but smile.

"Hold still," he says, his voice suddenly soft. "You have some glitter, right … here." He brushes my cheek, and his touch sends my pulse racing. I close my eyes as he tries to wipe the flakes away. The stuff is ubiquitous. The gallery has kids' classes on Saturday mornings, and my mom claims no amount of cleaning can eradicate it.

"Got it," he says finally.

I open my eyes, and his face is so close to mine, I catch my breath. "Thank you." I pull away and wipe my cheek, partly as a distraction and partly to try to erase the feeling of his hand on it. It doesn't quite work. "Now," I say, "let me see your masterpiece."

He returns to his own easel and flips his board around. "It's not finished yet."

"Come on. Show me."

"Not today. Someday."

"When?"

"When it's finished."

"Now who's worried about perfection?"

"Not me." He nods toward my board. "I'm like your flower. Reaching. It's all about the reaching."

"Right. For perfection."

He shakes his head. "That's where you're wrong. And anyway, who decides what's perfect and what's not? Certainly not me."

I am tempted to agree that someone like him wouldn't understand perfection, but I can't think of a way to do so without sounding mean, so instead I change the subject. "Want to hear the idea I have for our English project?"

Darius rubs his chin. "Let me guess. Instead of saying, 'A rose by any other name would smell as sweet,' we'll have a nose emoji and a rose emoji?"

I stick out my tongue. "The emojis are going to be a huge hit, you'll see. But that's not my idea. Actually, I was thinking we might want to start off with a brief live vignette to set the scene."

"Oh?" He sits up straighter on his stool. "With actual dialogue and acting?"

"Yes, but 'brief' is the key word."

"Okay. What are you thinking?"

"I could be talking to a friend—another prom queen candidate—and you walk up and try to get my attention, but we shut you down. Then we could switch to the video with the all the texts. It would give them some context."

He nods. "That works."

"Cool." I pick up a nearby paint sponge and squeeze it as though it's one of those stress balls. "So how do you want to do this? Should I write up my lines first and send them to you?" *Squeeze. Squeeze.* "Or maybe I can just write up the whole thing."

"The whole thing? Don't you trust me?" His voice teases, but something in his eyes tells me he suspects—fears—that he could be right.

"It's not that." I avoid his gaze. "I just thought it might be easier if—"

He reaches over and stills my hand. "I'm not worried about it being easy. I think we should work together on it."

I try to ignore the fact that for the second time in less than an hour, I am semi-holding-hands with Darius Groves.

"Hey." My mom calls to us from the front of the room, where she's cleaning a set of paintbrushes. "Less flirting, more art-ing back there."

I pull my hand away, my face burning. "We're not flirting, Mom. We're talking about schoolwork." I turn to him. "Come on. Let me write it. This is like a get-out-of-jail-free card for you."

Darius grins and leans toward me, his voice low. "Love goes toward love as schoolboys from their books, but love from love, toward school with heavy looks."

I feel my jaw drop. "Um. What?"

He laughs. "It's from the scene. Haven't you read it?"

"Of course. I mean, I skimmed it. I basically know what happens."

"I see. You skimmed it, though not well enough so that you even recognize a line from it. Yet you think I should let you write the retelling by yourself?"

My cheeks burn. "I'm planning to read it. Obviously."

"Please do. And then we'll write the retelling. Together. As a team."

I paste on a smile. "Fine. Together it is."

Chapter FIFTEEN

Maggs disentangles her right hand from my near-perfect Princess Leia bun and points at the print of "Luncheon of the Boating Party" propped up on my shelf. "Where'd you get that?"

"Oh, it's just something from the gallery gift shop." I avoid her eyes.

"It doesn't quite match the rest of your décor."

She's right. Renoir has a different aesthetic than my *Welcome to Night Vale* and *Stranger Things* posters. I'm not sure what made me decide to buy it after the class the other day. Or rather, I'm not sure I want to think about why I decided to buy it. I shrug. "It's a cool scene, that's all."

Maggs doesn't press it. I haven't told her about running into Darius or about the class. I don't want her opinion on the matter, regardless of whether it is pro- or anti-Darius. I need some time to figure out my own opinion first.

"There. Perfect." Maggs steps back and admires her handiwork.

I pick up my blaster rifle from my bed and strike a pose.

Maggs laughs and grabs her keys, heading toward my bedroom door. "I'll meet you at Jack's. I need to get ready."

"I can't wait to see your costume. Are you going for Earth Child or will it be more Psychedelia?"

Maggs pauses in the doorway. "Didn't I tell you? I decided against the hippie idea."

"What?"

"Too obvious." She grins. "I'm going as Katy Perry during her Cleopatra phase."

"Katy—Cleo—what the ... ?" I stare in disbelief at her retreating back.

"You'll love it!" she calls over her shoulder.

"I'm sure I will." I force a laugh as I pull out my phone and text Aiden.

Alicea: Forget hippie plan. Do you happen to have a Mark Antony costume lying around?

Ty is dressed as a prisoner and Becca as a sexy cop. She looks amazing, but her handcuff jokes make me want to use her plastic billy club on her. Or better yet, my blaster.

Maggs is running late, so I lurk in a corner of Jack's living room for a solid ten minutes trying to work up the nerve to walk up to them. Ty's laughter carries over the crowd and across the room. How I miss that sound. How I miss being the one to make him make that sound. Stupid handcuff jokes.

"The force be with you." A guy wearing a fireman's hat and carrying a garden hose steps into my line of vision. I recognize him as Grand View's goalie.

"And also with you," I say.

He looks confused.

"Get it? It's … never mind. Church humor."

"Right." He frowns, shakes his head, and walks away. Not exactly the confidence-booster I need at the moment, but I take a deep breath and a swig of my soda and force my feet to move toward them. I snagged the invite to this stupid party, made the costume, and sat through an hour of bun-rolling. I plan to make darn sure Ty sees me in all my Princess Leia glory.

"Hey, guys," I say, my voice unnaturally chipper. "Cute costumes. Very clever."

"Well, hello, Alicea." Becca gives me a once-over and leans into Ty. "Is that your real hair?" She reaches up to touch one of my buns, but I swat her hand away and turn to Ty.

"So what are you in for, troublemaker?" Again with the uber-perky voice.

Ty grins. "Good question."

"Isn't it obvious? Killer good looks," Becca says, planting a kiss on his cheek.

Ty laughs, grabs her badge, and pulls her in for a real kiss.

Eww. Not how this was supposed to go. My phone buzzes, so I mumble a "see you later" and turn to make my escape, though I'm not sure either of them notices. Maybe coming here wasn't such a brilliant idea.

It's Maggs, letting me know she's on her way. Thank goodness. Now where is Aiden? I text him to meet me in the kitchen.

As I stand at the counter, soda in hand, trying to decide whether to spike it with one of the many options lined up before me, I hear my name.

"Alicea. What are you doing?" It's Abi, and she's glaring at me. She's dressed as Tinkerbell, and she looks mischievous, sassy, and adorable.

"I was just thinking maybe some rum would—"

"No. It wouldn't." She wedges herself between me and the liquor and waves her star-tipped wand at my cup. "No boy is worth getting drunk over. Tell her, Roland."

Captain Hook has appeared in the doorway. He raises both hands—or rather a hand and a hook—and shakes his head. "Leave me out of this." Muttering something about how he prefers wrestling crocodiles to girl talk, he pivots—and, with a dramatic swoop of his cape—disappears.

Abi emits an exaggerated sigh. "See what I mean? Boys. Anyway, this isn't about your beverage selection. It's about you showing up here in that Princess Leia outfit. Super cute, by the way. But I see what you're doing. You're still hung up on Ty, aren't you?"

I glance around to make sure no one can hear. "Can you blame me?"

"Yes, actually, I can. He dumped you a week before prom

and has been serial dating ever since. What part of that do you find attractive?"

I tap my blaster rifle against my leg. I don't need this from Abi. I get it enough from Brie. And from Maggs, who never actually says anything but I can tell is silently judge-y about it.

None of them understands.

They have no idea what it's like to be mired in obscurity while secretly crushing on someone for years. A year ago, I was mostly hanging out on programming boards with people with names like WebNinjaBabe and ByteMeBrett. Getting a few "likes" on one of my posts constituted the pinnacle of my popularity, until one day, as I grabbed my pre-calc book out of my locker, I turned around to find the object of my obsession standing behind me holding a candy cane and asking if I'd like to go to a movie Friday night, and everything finally, incredibly, inconceivably fell into place for four and a half glorious months.

"You think I don't understand?" Abi seems to have read my mind. "Trust me, I get it. Briggsy and I have had our ups and downs, but I'm here to tell you that having a boyfriend is only worth it if he's the *right* boyfriend. You can't settle."

Settle? Is she insane? Dating Ty Walker would not be settling. Quite the opposite. "Listen, I appreciate the advice, but I know what I'm doing."

"Do you? Because I think you're—"

She doesn't have a chance to finish, because at that moment Aiden appears at her side. He's wearing a white shirt unbuttoned halfway down his chest, a shiny black suit jacket, and sunglasses. His hair is slicked back with some kind of weird grease, and he's holding a microphone. "What do you think?" he asks.

I shake my head. "I think I'm confused. Who are you supposed to be?"

"Marc Anthony. Come on. I look exactly like him. Well, except my hairline isn't receding yet."

I groan. "But that's—"

"Hold on. Check this out." He pulls what I assume is supposed to be a smoldering gaze and belts out the first few lines of "I Need to Know."

I snatch the microphone out of his hand. "Aiden. Not Marc Anthony. Mark *Antony*. As in, the Roman guy. As in Antony and Cleopatra."

"Oh, crap." Aiden's eyes flash with panic. "I figured maybe Maggs was coming as J Lo. So she's Cleopatra?"

"Well, she's Katy Perry dressed as Cleopatra, but, yeah."

Abi laughs and walks a three-sixty around Aiden. "Forget it. You make a hot Marc Anthony. Go out there and own it."

"What? No." I point at her. "You're the one who said we have to make Maggs think he's her destiny."

"Oh, man, this is a disaster." Aiden runs his hand through his hair. "Ugh." He groans as he holds out his shiny fingers toward me.

"Gross." I push him toward the sink. "What is that stuff, anyway?"

"Coconut oil. It was all I could find. My mom uses it on her face."

Abi leans in and sniffs his head. "Yum. Coconut-y."

Aiden washes his hands and dries them on his pants. "Let's forget this whole thing. It's hopeless."

"Wait!" I grab his arm as he starts to leave. "Maggs is going to be here any minute. You can't let one little misunderstanding ruin everything."

He shakes his head. "It's not just that. It's Maggs. She'll never notice a guy like me, and even if she does, how long would it last? A week? Two weeks?"

"That's not necessarily true. Not if it's meant to be. If two people belong together, they'll end up together." I'm not sure whether I'm trying to convince him or myself. "Listen. I have an idea." I sling my blaster rifle over my shoulder and motion to him and Abi. "Come on. Let's find Jack."

Chapter
SIXTEEN

"Strawberry Shortcake? Forget it." Aiden backs away from the bed sheet Jack is holding as though it's contaminated.

"Suit yourself." Jack tosses it onto a shelf in the linen closet and saunters away. We'd asked if he had something Aiden could use to create a toga. The only sheet he was willing to sacrifice belonged to his sister when she was eight.

"Come on. It's not that bad." I pick it up and unfold it. "If you wear it inside out, you can barely see the cartoons."

"Um. No." Aiden looks at me as though I'm crazy.

I turn to Abi for support, but even she appears skeptical.

Aiden points at me. "If you think I'm wearing that, you're insane. And you are the worst Boyfriend Whisperer ever." He backs away slowly, then turns and runs as though Strawberry Shortcake and I are conspiring to jeopardize his manhood.

As he rounds the corner of the hallway, he smashes into

Maggs, who tumbles backward on her heels until he catches her.

"Oh my gosh, I'm so sorry." He steadies her, his eyes wide. "You're ... wow. Great costume."

Maggs looks stunning in a beaded dress, with a series of tiny bejeweled braids framing her face and dark black liner forming dramatic dips and swirls around her eyes. Very exotic. "Thanks," she says. "Who are you?"

Aiden's expression falls. "You don't know? Seriously? You don't recognize me?"

She shakes her head. "Sorry."

He turns and continues down the hallway, calling over his shoulder. "Aiden. Aiden Jackson. You sat next to me in civics last year."

"That's not ... " Maggs starts to call after him, but he's already disappeared into the next room. She turns to Abi and me. "That wasn't what I meant. Of course I know he's Aiden. I just don't know who he's dressed as."

"He's supposed to be Mark Anthony. Minus the receding hairline."

"Oh." Maggs looks perplexed, which I suppose makes sense, because who goes to a Halloween party dressed as a middle-aged pop star? She points to the sheet, which I'm still holding. "What's that for?"

Abi laughs and eases the sheet from my grip. "It's nothing. It's ... holy crap. How did I not notice that earlier?" She points to Maggs's elaborate headdress, which has a huge rubber asp coiled up in it. "I'm going to need you to keep your distance."

Everyone knows Abi is terrified of snakes. Rumor has it

one got into her car last year, and she almost drove off the road when she saw it. Still, I suspect her alarm is at least partly feigned—a diversion—because as she's talking, she balls up the sheet, throws it into the linen closet, slams the door, and takes off down the hallway.

"Well. That seemed extreme." Maggs frowns as she watches Abi's retreating figure.

"You look amazing," I say. I reach up and finger one of her braids.

"Thanks. Your buns are holding up nicely."

I smile, but Maggs sees through it.

"Sorry about Ty and Becca. They look ridiculous."

"She literally has him chained to her. Which I'm pretty sure is not proper police protocol."

"Nothing about that girl is proper." Maggs grabs my hand and leads me back toward the party. "It'll pass. His flings always do. Forget about those two and let's enjoy the party."

But I don't. I don't enjoy it at all. Both of my missions tonight have failed, I've been labeled the "Worst Boyfriend Whisperer Ever," and these stupid side buns are starting to give me a headache. My only consolation is knowing I have an entire survey full of Ty's deepest thoughts and secrets at home waiting to be explored and exploited. Princess Leia didn't let a whole army of Stormtroopers stop her from achieving her missions, and I'm certainly not going to let Faux-Officer Becca Marsh keep me from mine.

Chapter
SEVENTEEN

Cuppa Joe is packed on Sunday afternoon. I'm supposed to meet Darius here to work on our project, but the only seat available is a loveseat covered with pink and blue hearts in a back corner. *Wonderful.* I decide to hang out by the door for a few minutes to see if anyone leaves. The elderly couple sitting near the register look as though they're almost done, and the kid with the earphones zoning out by the window appears to have finished his coffee hours ago. *Would it be rude to—*

"Hello, Bright Angel." Darius's voice startles me.

"Hey."

"Ready to declare how much we heart each other?" He puts his hands together in a heart shape and flashes a goofy smile.

My cheeks grow warm, so I glance away. Unfortunately,

my gaze falls squarely on the loveseat.

"Ah, perfect." Darius says, offering a dramatic wave toward it. "Shall we?"

I paste on a smile. He wants to see me squirm, and I refuse to give him the satisfaction. "If thou thinkest I am too quickly won, I'll frown, and be perverse, and say thee nay."

His eyebrows shoot up. "Someone's finally read the scene." He places his hand on the small of my back and guides me toward the seat. "Can I get you a coffee, or maybe some hot chocolate?"

I look at him in surprise. "Sure. Though I'll take a chai. Hazelnut, please."

I watch as he walks to the counter and places our order. The barista laughs at something he says, and he pushes the ever-falling shock of hair away from his eyes. Outside of school, he seems less like a misfit. It makes me uneasy. The fact is, I have no idea who Darius Groves is. Is he the smartass from my calc and lit classes? Is he the idiot who was expelled from his last school for fighting and nearly suspended at ours for pulling a guy's shorts down? Is he the aspiring artist who embraces imperfection? Or is he the charmer buying me a chai tea and chatting up the barista while he waits for our order?

And how the heck did I get matched with any of the above?

"Here you go, Bright Angel." Darius sets a steaming cup in front of me.

"Thanks. And please stop calling me that."

He feigns an innocent expression. "Why, pray tell?"

I roll my eyes and groan. "You are so sixteenth century."

"So you prefer 'hottie.'"

"What? No." I kick him, which is a mistake because it emphasizes how close we are sitting on the too-cozy loveseat. "Let's get this over with." I scooch to the edge of the seat and power up my tablet. "Abi has agreed to help with the first scene, the one where you come up and try to talk to me. After she shuts you down, we can turn on the slide show with the texts."

"Sounds good." Darius nods. "I think you should text me first. You know—apologizing for your friend's rude behavior. You could maybe find a 'sorry' emoji."

I glare.

"What?"

"You agreed to do the texts. I agreed to go with your idea of the prom queen and the loser. It's called a compromise. So you don't get to keep mocking the texts."

Darius's teasing grin fades, and his eyes soften. "You're right. I'm sorry. I promise I'll stop." Just as I start to believe he means it, he pulls the sides of his mouth down and bugs his eyes in an exaggerated frown-y face.

I can't help but laugh. "You're such a jerk."

"Yeah. But I made you LOL."

"Shut up." I'm not sure which annoys me more, the fact that he's ridiculing me, or the fact that he's making me laugh at him ridiculing me.

We spend the next hour roughing out our script. He mostly refrains from mocking, and I have to admit, he does come up with some good lines. Once we're finished, I offer to type up the slides and create a PowerPoint presentation.

"That would be great," he says. "Why don't you send

them to me for a final proof?"

I eye him warily. "A final proof? Meaning, so you can take out all the awesome emojis?"

"I will take out zero emojis." He pulls a super-serious expression and holds up three fingers. "You have nothing to fear. Scout's honor."

"Fine." I shut down my tablet. "I'll send you the slides. And thanks again for the tea." I smile and wave goodbye as I weave through the tables toward the door, but the chai churns in my stomach. Because Darius Groves is many things, but I'm guessing a Boy Scout is not one of them.

Chapter
EIGHTEEN

Grand View's gym during the girls' basketball season opener is as loud as a freight train. Lexi is one of the top forwards in the country and has led our team to the state championship game for the past three years. Tonight we're playing our rivals, Pine Bridge.

Maggs, Brie, and I came straight from our Tuesday afternoon dance class. As we stroll down the edge of the court searching for a spot in the packed bleachers, I scan the crowd for Ty. I can't help myself. It's a compulsion, like checking my phone for texts after the bell.

Finally, Maggs points toward an opening at the end of the court. "We can sit over there."

"Cool. Let's grab—" The words catch in my throat as I notice who's sitting just above the empty spot. Darius. I haven't told Maggs or Brie yet about running into him at the gallery or about meeting up with him at Cuppa Joe. Neither of those were a big deal. One was a total accident and the other was for a school project—a project I have also somehow failed to mention to either of them.

"Ooh, yes, that's perrrrfect." Brie glances at me, and I'm not sure which are wider, her eyes or her grin. She rushes up the steps before I can protest.

"Oops. Sorry." Maggs offers an apologetic smile. "I didn't see him sitting there."

Wonderful. I trudge up the steps, semi-hiding behind Maggs. Maybe Darius will want to ignore me as much as I want to ignore him. Or maybe he'll at least have sense enough to play it super casual. Say hi and leave it at that.

"Hey, Bright Angel," he calls before I even reach the seat. I swear he couldn't have shouted it any louder if he'd had a megaphone.

Brie and Maggs both stop and turn to stare at me.

Omigod. I glare at him and am about to say something very rude and perhaps slightly crude and *definitely* not family-friendly when I notice the little girl sitting beside him. She appears to be about nine or ten years old.

My mouth snaps shut.

"Why did he call you that?" the girl asks, studying me with great interest.

"Isn't it obvious?" Darius answers for me. He places one hand over his heart and reaches the other toward me. "Those eyes, two of the fairest stars in all the heavens. Her cheeks, so bright they would—"

I slap his hand away. "We're doing a project together. For school. He's teasing." I glance at Maggs and Brie as I take my seat, my expression daring them to utter a word.

"My brother loves to tease." The girl scooches down a row and squeezes between Maggs and me. "I'm Jaycee. What's your name?"

"Hey, kiddo." Darius taps her on the shoulder. "Get back up here."

"It's okay," I assure him. I smile at her. "I'm Alicea."

She extends her hand, and I shake it. "Nice to meet you, Alicea," she says. "I love basketball."

"Oh? Do you play?"

Jaycee nods. "I'm a forward. Like Lexi."

"Ahhh, so you're a Lexi fan?"

She nods again, her eyes wide. "She's, like, a total baller. She's one of the best in the whole country."

"She sure is."

"Do you know her?"

"I do."

Jaycee's eyes grow big. "For real?"

"Yep."

"Think you could introduce me to her?"

"Jacqueline." Darius tugs at the back of her shirt.

"She's fine," I tell him. I turn back to Jaycee. "We can try to catch her after the game, before she goes to the locker room."

"Ooh." She looks back at her brother. "Can we, please?"

Darius gives me a smile so warm, genuine, and unlike the smirk I'm used to seeing that—for a moment—I forget how much he annoys me. "We'll see," he says. "If you can manage not to pester us for the next four quarters and listen to everything I say."

Jaycee squeals and moves back up to sit beside him.

He winks at me, which—fortunately—neither Maggs nor Brie witnesses. I twist back around in my seat and try my best to ignore him. Still, I can't help but soften a bit as I overhear him reviewing the finer points of the game with his sister. Whether it's the positioning of a player's arms or feet, or a defense formation, or a skill shot, he offers a running commentary explaining to her what works and what doesn't. He seems to really know his stuff.

At halftime, Maggs and Brie practically drag me down the bleachers, across the court, and into a hallway.

"Are you kidding me?"

"Bright Angel?"

"What school project?"

"You've been holding out on us, girl."

I wave my hands in front of my face to fend off the verbal onslaught. "I have not been holding out," I say. "It's nothing. It's a stupid English lit project, and it's mostly just texts, and we've had to meet a couple of times to plan it, but I swear it's no big deal. After Friday it'll all be over and we can get back to our normal lives."

"You've had to meet?" A grin spreads across Brie's face. "You're blushing," she says. "How did Darius put it? 'Cheeks bright they would … ' what? I don't believe you let him finish."

"Shame those stars, as daylight doth a lamp," I mumble.

"Ah, yes, the stars being your eyes," Maggs chimes in.

I glare at them both. "It's from *Romeo and Juliet*. We're doing a modern-day retelling, and like I said, it'll be mostly texts."

"*Romeo and Juliet*?" Brie is bouncing on her heels. "Are you kidding me? That's so romantic. It's—"

"No. It's not. It's not romantic. It's an assignment. For a

class. And this conversation is over." I turn on my heel and stomp back toward the gym. As I walk through the double doors, I literally run into Ty and Becca.

"Excuse me." Becca pulls away from their lip lock and shoots me a dirty look. "Watch where you're going."

Ty raises an eyebrow but says nothing.

I wish I were bold enough to remark on how inadvisable it is to stop and suck face in the middle of the gym doorway during halftime of a sold-out game, but instead I offer a thin smile. "Sorry," I mumble as I make my escape back to the bleachers.

I try to enjoy the second half, but my run-in with Ty and Becca has left an ache in the pit of my stomach. I remember how it once felt to kiss Ty.

Our first kiss was in the parking lot at Italiano's. It was our first date—a Ryan Gosling flick followed by flatbread pizza and wings. The night had been perfect, and as we walked back to Ty's car, he reached over for my hand. He opened the passenger-side door for me but then turned and placed his free hand on the frame, blocking my path. My heart raced, and I leaned into him. He brushed a strand of hair away from my face, placing it with care behind my ear.

"You're adorable when you eat pizza, you know that?" He touched the edge of my lip with his thumb. "The way you nibble at the cheese."

I blushed at that, and he laughed. "It's true," he said. "As I sat there watching you battle that mozzarella, all I could think about was how much I wanted to do this." He tilted my chin up toward him and pressed his lips against mine, softly at first and then more intensely. It was my first real kiss, and while I'd expected it to be wet and weird and maybe a little clumsy, it was none of those things. It was almost like breathing—normal and natural and simple. I leaned my full weight into Ty's chest, and he emitted a low moan deep in his throat.

"WOOHOO!"

A roar and a loud buzz bring me back to the game. I blink and check the scoreboard. Time has run out with Grand View up by two points. Apparently Lexi scored a three-pointer at the buzzer to clinch the win.

"Game over." Jaycee is beside me in a flash, her eyes shining. "Can we meet Lexi now? Please?"

I smile and nod, and when I glance back at Darius, he mouths *thank you*. I grab Jaycee's hand and lead her down to the court, with Darius close behind us.

The crowd has surged onto the floor, swarming the team, so it takes forever to reach the Grand View bench. I spot Lexi's ponytail a few feet ahead of us when someone taps my shoulder and calls my name.

It's Aiden. "Hey. A bunch of us are heading over to McDonald's. Do you and Maggs want to come?"

I glance around and lean toward him. Even though my mouth is about two inches from his ear, I have to shout to be heard above the din. "Define 'a bunch of us.'"

Aiden gives me a side-eye. "Milo, Jack, Fernando, Ty, and maybe—"

"Okay, sure. Give me a minute." I turn back to Jaycee. "Hold on a second, sweetheart. I need to text Maggs about something." I sense Darius frowning at me from the periphery, but I ignore him. I text Maggs and Brie, who say they'll come.

"We're on," I say to Aiden. "We'll catch up with you over there."

He pumps his fist in the air, and as I turn back toward the team, I realize they're retreating toward the locker rooms.

"Shoot." I leave Jaycee and Darius behind as I try to chase them down through the crowd.

"Lexi!" I shout, but she doesn't hear me. "Lexi, hold up."

If I miss her, we're screwed. No one is allowed into the locker rooms—not parents, not friends, and certainly not a tween-age fan accompanied by a random student.

I weave in and out through the crowd, following the team across the court, but I'm too late. The girls disappear one by one through the locker room doors. *Darn it.* I turn to find Jaycee making her way toward me, but she stops and the light fades from her eyes as she realizes we've missed our chance.

"I'm so sorry," I say when I reach her.

"It's okay. You tried." Jaycee offers a smile, but it doesn't hide her disappointment.

"You know, they'll come back out in about twenty or thirty—"

Darius shakes his head. "It's a school night. I need to get her home."

"Right." *Ugh.* "I feel so bad. I'm sorry. I just … Aiden asked me something, and … " I'm not sure how to finish that sentence. *And I totally ditched on the promise I made you.*

Darius shrugs. "No worries." He rests his hand on Jaycee's shoulder. "Maybe next time, Jay."

She nods. "Maybe."

As they turn to leave, I call goodbye.

Darius turns back and winks. Only this time it's minus the warm smile.

Chapter NINETEEN

LIBBY Question #19: You prefer your date to be:
- A. Smart
- B. Athletic
- C. Funny
- D. Flirty

Ty picked "D." Which explains his attraction to Becca, I suppose. And which is why I'm sitting across the booth from him at McDonald's giggling hysterically as he tells a story about how his Eagle Scout project—a set of benches he built and painted for his church's picnic area—went awry because of an unexpected storm. Meanwhile, Brie rolls her eyes at me from the next table.

"Too bad McD's doesn't serve flatbread." I lean forward

and pout my lips in an effort to remind him of my cheese-nibbling prowess.

Ty grimaces. "Pretty sure McDonald's flatbread would be disgusting." He takes a swig of his soda and munches on a piece of ice.

"So where's Becca?" I hate to bring her up, but I can't help myself.

He shrugs. "She didn't want to come. Said all the shouting at the game gave her a headache."

I nod. He doesn't seem overly concerned. Perhaps they're not as serious as I'd feared?

"That's too bad. It did get pretty loud. Especially when Lexi scored that final basket." I point a chicken nugget at him. "Remember the game-winning goal you scored in the Richmond tournament last spring? That was amazing."

"I figured that dude would go left." Ty leans back in his seat, his eyes shining at the memory. "He went left, like, seventy percent of the time. I liked my odds."

"It was a beautiful kick." We'd been over that shot many times. I always loved that Ty approached soccer as much as a mental game as a physical one. And that he was so often right.

He reaches over to grab the nugget, which I've forgotten I'm still holding, and pops it into his mouth. "Those were some good times, weren't they?"

My heart pounds. "Do you think about those times much?"

"Course I do, Al."

I smile. *Al.* My brother and his friends called me that when I was little and I hated it, but coming from Ty, that single syllable is perfection.

"Know what I miss the most?" he asks.

I shake my head.

"I miss how we used to—"

"Yo, Alicea." Aiden plops down next to Ty, cutting him off. "You gotta help me. Milo is monopolizing Maggs over there. How am I supposed to get her attention if I can't even get a word in?"

"Aiden, do you mind? We're having a conversation." I glare, hoping he'll leave, but once again, I've underestimated his persistence.

"Give me something, anything," he pleads. "Her favorite movie or book or song. What does she love more than anything in the world?"

I peer over at Maggs. She's giving Milo her flirty eyes. *Crap.* "Um. I don't know. Daisies?"

Aiden gives me a side-eye. "Daisies? As in, the flower?"

"Yeah. She really likes them."

"What am I supposed to do with that?"

"I don't know. You're putting me on the spot here."

"Know what you call a guy who's dating Maggs?" Ty asks him.

"What?"

"Her Next Ex."

Aiden glowers, and I kick Ty under the table. "This is different."

"How?"

"Because Aiden is her match. Libby says so." My stomach clenches as I utter the words. What does Libby know? What if she has no idea what she's talking about? Or worse, what if she does?

"Well, if she's your match, why are you asking Alicea for help? Shouldn't you be into all the same stuff?"

"Ty has a point," I say. "Talk to her about the things you like. You like art, right? I mean, you knew about that de Kooning guy."

Aiden nods.

"Maggs likes that dude who did the painting of the girl sitting on the hill. You know the one. It's really ... orange."

"You mean Wyeth? 'Christina's World'?"

"Yeah. Maybe."

Aiden shakes his head. "Thanks. I think. Wish me luck."

I lean forward and offer Ty another nugget as Aiden takes off. "Now, where were we? I believe you were saying something about what you miss the—"

Ty's phone dings, and he pulls it out of his front shirt pocket. "Becca."

Of course. I slump back into my seat as he texts her back, waits for her reply, then texts her back again. Wash, rinse, repeat, repeat, repeat. I give a loud sigh and slurp at the bottom of my soda, but he seems not to notice. Whatever. Apparently, I am doomed to live the rest of my days on earth never knowing what Ty misses most about our almost-five-months together.

Finally, he sticks his phone back in his pocket and looks up. "You know what? I should head home," he says. "I've got a physics quiz first period."

"Right. Me too. I mean, not the part about the quiz, but the part about going home."

"Okay, well, see you later." He stands to go.

"Ty?"

"Yeah?"

"I, um, just wanted to remind you. This Saturday? It's the dance recital. I'm leading the corps, and so … it's not really a big deal, but you seemed interested, so if you want to come, you could. It starts at three."

Ty nods. "Okay, sure. I mean, I have some soccer stuff this weekend, so no promises, but if I can make it, I will."

I let out a breath I hadn't realized I'd been holding. "Great. That'd be awesome."

"Cool." And with that, he saunters off into the night.

Chapter
TWENTY

I'm a bit nervous when I walk into lit class on Friday. I've successfully avoided contact with Darius since dashing his kid sister's dreams on Tuesday. Now, not only do I have to face him, I have to play Juliet to his modern-day Romeo.

"Ready to do this thing?" Abi greets me as I sit down at my desk.

I offer what I hope comes off as a confident smile as I reach into my backpack, find the flash drive with the slideshow, and hand it to Mr. Dunham. He takes the drive from me and slips it into his laptop port, but as he starts to copy the file, Darius appears at his side.

"Use this one instead." Darius hands him his own drive. "I had a few edits."

Uh-oh. I don't like the sound of that. "Wait. What edits?"

"Nothing major." Darius's tone is dismissive as he passes

me on his way to his seat, but I notice he doesn't make eye contact. Shoot. What has he done?

I don't have time to question him, because the bell rings and Mr. Dunham calls up the first pair of students to perform their retelling. Ty and Jack recreate the *Don Quixote* windmill scene, and their version is every bit as bizarre as the original, only instead of windmills, Ty is battling a make-believe defective oilrig, and I guess it's supposed to make some kind of environmental statement, though I'm not sure exactly what. Next up are Abi and Briggs, and their *Cyrano* scene is beyond adorable. Anyone can see they're perfect for each other.

Three more pairs get up and act out scenes based on *Pride and Prejudice*, *A Tale of Two Cities*, and *Of Mice and Men*. All the while, I'm getting more and more nervous. When will it be our turn? And what were Darius's edits? Finally, Mr. Dunham glances at his chart. "Alicea and Darius. You're on."

The beginning of our skit goes exactly as scripted. Abi and I stand at the front of the room, squealing about our plans for prom. It's totally over the top, and Abi uses a super annoying high-pitched voice that makes everyone laugh in all the right places.

Darius approaches us. "Excuse me. Can I talk to Juliet for a minute?" His eyes meet mine for the first time since the basketball game. Thank goodness this is supposed to be the awkward part of the scene, because my face burns under his gaze.

Abi offers her best mean-girl once-over. "Hello? Can't you see we're in the middle of a very important convo? And shouldn't you be hanging out at the skate park with all your juvie friends?"

Darius mumbles an apology and shuffles away. After Abi and I say our goodbyes, I pull out my phone and pretend to type. I reach over to dim the lights, cue Mr. D. to start the slideshow, and sit back down at my desk.

The slides start out fine, popping up one text at a time, starting with my apology and moving on to some flirting, with plenty of emojis. As planned, Romeo eventually gets up the nerve to tell Juliet why he wanted to talk to her.

```
Romeo: Heard you discussing prom.
Juliet: Yeah.
Romeo: Still no date?
Juliet. :P
Juliet. Don't go there.
Juliet: You know it'll never work.
Romeo: I haven't even asked yet.
Juliet: Let's keep it that way.
Juliet. Please.
Romeo: Why?
Juliet: You know the answer to that. We're
from different worlds.
Romeo: So this is it? We just text forever?
Juliet: :(
```

At this point, Romeo is supposed to say that texting isn't enough, that he wants to hear Juliet's voice and hold her hand in his, but instead of the next slide, a video appears.

What the—? This can't be good. Resisting the urge to turn and glare at Darius, I slip down in my seat and brace myself for his unauthorized "edits."

Darius's face appears on the screen, a hip-hop beat playing in the background, and he begins to rap.

Oh, Juliet, sweet Juliet,
Don't hide behind that crown.
Give me a chance
At the senior dance.
My love won't let you down.

You're posing on your balcony,
Your pedestal, afraid of me,
Your royalty's a fantasy
And vanity's your enemy.
Well, pardon me, your majesty.
If I don't bow on bended knee
Because, fair lady, I can see
The maiden you are meant to be.

At this point, the camera pans out, and Darius starts dancing—a few simple moves, but I have to give him credit. He's a natural. He has what Ms. DuBois would call "*savoir faire* of the hips." And all the while, he keeps rapping.

Oh, Juliet, sweet Juliet,
You think you have it made.
That's very well,
But can't you tell,
It's all a masquerade?

Look closely there into their eyes,

A cloying charm is their disguise.
I pledge to you a thousand times,
You are not wise to compromise
Your future for a pack of lies.
In fact, I would hypothesize
Your regal court is your demise
Because with them, your spirit dies.

Oh, Juliet, sweet Juliet,
Hark now and hear my plea.
Don't be proud.
Come off your cloud.
And take the floor with me.

Come, fair lady, don't be blue.
I'll tell you now what you should do
You must eschew your haughty crew
And come with me. My love is true.
Your balcony may have a view
But now it's time to come down to
Your Romeo. I'm someone who
In life and death will honor you.

Oh, Juliet, sweet Juliet,
You are my angel bright.
In tux and gown, we'll hit the town.
Say you'll be mine tonight.

As the music fades, Darius backs away from the camera, signing off with, "Promposal. Shakespeare style."

The entire class breaks out in applause as someone hits the lights. I stay tucked down in my seat, frozen. At no point did we ever mention a video, much less a rap scene. Darius totally lied when he insisted he wanted to work together as a team and when he said that I had nothing to fear and claimed his changes were "nothing major." That wasn't really a retelling; it was more of a weird Elizabethan-Kanye-style mashup, and I have no idea what it'll do to our grade.

But none of that is what bothers me most. What bothers me most is that although my head is cursing Darius for going off script, my heart can't help but admit that that video was H-O-T hot.

Chapter
TWENTY-ONE

"It's okay, sweetheart." I hug Kayla and stroke her dark curls as she cries into my leotard. The poor thing slipped and fell halfway through *Frere Jacque* and ran sobbing off the stage. I know exactly how she feels, though when you make a fool of yourself in front of hundreds of people at age three, it's slightly cuter than when you're sixteen.

"Go ahead, dear," Ms. DuBois urges her. "Finish up. You'll be fine."

Kayla glances out at her fellow Tip Toe Toddlers in their pink-and-purple tutus, flitting around each other like butterflies in a field, and turns back to me, wide-eyed. I wipe a tear from her cheek and give her another quick squeeze. "Ms. DuBois is right," I tell her. "You'll be fine. You've got this. Besides, look at Ginny." I point to a little redhead who is busy doing deep *pliés* while everyone else is twirling. "She's lost without you beside her."

That seems to do the trick. Kayla sniffs, gives a determined nod, and rushes back out to her spot, tapping Ginny's shoulder and urging her to twirl.

"Thank you, Alicea." Ms. DuBois offers a grateful smile. "I appreciate your help, but what are you doing up here? You should be downstairs stretching with the Seniors. Your group takes the stage in twenty minutes."

"Yes, ma'am." I flee toward the stairs. I was backstage for two reasons, both of which have to do with boys and neither of which I wish to share with Ms. DuBois. First, I needed a break from Brie, Maggs, and half the girls in the corps. Apparently Darius and his rap are the talk of the school, and everyone wants to hear how it went down. Since I have yet to piece together my own feelings about it, I've been brushing them off with shrugs and vague replies. Second, I decided to peek through the crack in the curtain to see whether Ty might be in the audience. Did he make it, or did his "soccer stuff" keep him away?

When I reach the bottom step, I crumple against the wall. Because Ty's not here; I scoured the crowd and didn't see him. I did, however, see one face that surprised me: Aiden Jackson, holding a bouquet of daisies. The boy's got guts. He never did get a chance to talk to Maggs the other night at McDonald's. Part of me thinks his showing up here is the sweetest thing ever; the other part can't help but be jealous. Why can't I be more like Maggs, with boys chasing after me with flowers? Not to mention, I'm well aware that Aiden and Ty are teammates, and apparently "soccer stuff" didn't keep *him* away.

Is Brie right? Do I try to make things into something they're not when it comes to Ty? Is it possible that where Ty and I are concerned, "maybe" really *does* mean "probably not"?

I exhale as the applause washes over us. Somehow I managed to pull myself together and get my head into the dance. Heather broke form ever so briefly on her *pas de chat*, but otherwise the corps was flawless. We sneak glances at each other and smile as we take our bows.

As we head offstage, I pull Brie aside and lower my voice. "Aiden Jackson is here."

"Okay. So?"

"He has flowers. Daisies, for Maggs." Her eyes widen, and I grab her hands in mine. "We need to help him out. Give him moral support, talk him up to her. Whatever we can do."

Brie's eyes narrow. "What do you care? I'm mean, I'm happy to do my part, but—"

"Libby matched them. I just want to help."

"Libby? I didn't think you—"

"I know. I don't. But … " But what? Why exactly am I doing this? Maybe I'm still hoping if I help Aiden, he'll do me a favor someday with Ty. Or maybe I like the idea of

Maggs dating a soccer player so we can hang out with the team. Or maybe it's like Lexi said and I want to make good on my Boyfriend Whisperer promise. Or maybe it's simply that Aiden actually seems super sweet and sincere, and he drenched his hair in coconut oil and brought daisies all in the name of love, which is pretty freaking romantic. "It's for Maggs," I say, finally. "And she loves daisies."

Brie screws up her lips and nods. "Okay. I'll do what I can."

"Do what you can about what?" Maggs appears at our side.

"About getting more height on my *brisé*." Brie doesn't miss a beat. Sometimes it scares me how easily that girl can lie when she needs to. "That was some awesome dancing out there, by the way. Seriously, Maggs, you rocked it."

She's pretty good at changing the subject, too.

I smile and nod in agreement. "Totally. Now, shall we go meet our adoring fans?"

"By 'adoring fans,' I assume you mean our parents?" Maggs asks.

"We'll see."

Brie and I each wrap our arms in hers and walk her out to the lobby. Sure enough, Aiden is standing there with his daisies, a look of terror in his eyes.

Maggs breaks away from us and runs over to her mom and dad. I give Aiden two thumbs up and a nod of encouragement, and Brie marches up to him. "I hope you know what you're doing."

I nudge her with my elbow, and she sighs. "The daisies are a good start. Go for it."

I smile and repeat the thumbs up. That was not exactly

the confidence booster I was hoping for from Brie, but if nothing else, she seems to have propelled the poor guy into action. He walks over to Maggs and holds out the daisies.

She turns to him, her expression a mixture of surprise and confusion. "Wow, thanks, Aiden!" She plucks a single daisy from his bouquet. "I adore daisies." She sticks it behind her ear. That's so sweet of you to give these out. Thanks again." And with that, she turns back to her parents, clearly oblivious to the dejected mass of nerves standing beside her.

Aiden retreats, his bouquet-minus-one in hand. I wave him over. Brie has already slipped away to find her parents and Blake, so I'm on my own now.

"Well, that was a total fail," he says, his posture as wilted as those daisies will be in about a week.

"No, it's not. First, she called you Aiden. I told you she knows your name. And second, she called you sweet. That's not nothing."

Aiden's eyes brighten a bit as I go on, convincing him that Maggs's misunderstanding about the daisies is actually a good thing—that it gives him a subtle base to build from and to have her eventually chase after him rather than the other way around. After all, guys chase after her all the time, and it never ultimately works out. Getting her to notice him like this might be just the ticket. I'm not sure I believe my pep talk myself, but it all sounds good.

"Maybe you're right," he says, finally.

"Of course I am." I take a daisy from him and gesture to the sea of leotards and tutus surrounding us. "Now start handing out the rest of these." I point to Kayla. "And make sure she gets two."

Chapter
TWENTY-TWO

I tap the tip of the compass spike over and over into my palm. Hard enough to feel its teeny prick, but not hard enough to draw blood. I'm hanging out in the supply closet next to my mother's classroom trying to convince myself that I drove out to the gallery tonight for a perfectly valid reason. After all, I do need to research types of presentation boards and adhesives for my Grand View Tech Fair project. I just happened to choose the night when Mom has her multi-media class to do it. And so what if the tech fair is more than two months away? A girl likes to be prepared.

I glance at my phone. Class breaks in five minutes. My mouth goes dry and my breath quickens. *Ouch.* And that jab was a little too hard. I toss the compass back into its box and emerge from the closet.

What should I do? Go to the gift shop? Pretend I'm

admiring the art along the walls? Hang out here as though I need to talk to my mom? For someone who likes to be prepared, I haven't really planned this part out very well. Not that "this" is anything. It's an innocent—

"Hey, Bright Angel." A full four minutes early, Darius appears in front of me, fresh out of class. He's wearing a plain white t-shirt and an olive hoodie that brings out tiny green flecks in his mostly blue eyes. He regards me warily. "You still talking to me?"

I've avoided him since our presentation, as much out of confusion as anger. I squint and place my hands on my hips. "I'm not big on surprises, you know."

"Sorry about that. But it was a good surprise, right? You can't tell me you didn't like it."

My lips twitch into a smile as I recall his "You are my angel bright" line, but I won't let him off so easily. "Whether I liked it isn't the issue. You went behind my back. If you wanted to do a rap, why didn't you tell me?"

He flashes one of his infuriating grins. "So you did like it."

I glare. "Don't avoid the question. Why didn't you tell me?"

"Come on, now. If I had told you I wanted to cut half of our texts and replace them with a rap video, would you have let me?"

I open my mouth, but nothing comes out. He's right. I wouldn't have.

"See? I figured it would be easier to ask forgiveness than permission." He leans his head down toward me and lowers his voice. "So do you?"

"Do I what?"

"Forgive me?"

"Well ... I ... " My breath catches in my throat, and my head suddenly feels light. I don't have a chance to answer because, at that moment, my mom bustles through the doorway and into the hall.

"Alicea, dear. What a nice surprise. What brings you here?"

I step back and blink hard. "Oh, I ... " I point in the general direction of the supply room door. "I needed to check out your students. I mean, supplies. For a project."

Mom glances from me to Darius and back again. "Mmhmm. Did you find what you were looking for?"

"Maybe. I mean, I'm not sure."

"I see. Well, focus a little and you will." She kisses the side of my forehead and heads toward the exit. "See you at home. No rush."

I stare at the floor, unable to meet Darius's gaze. "I owe you an apology, too, for the other night at the game. I felt horrible about that." I look up. "I definitely want to make it up to you and Jaycee, though. At the next home game."

Darius nods. "So does that mean we're even? As far as apologizing and forgiving?"

I smile, surprised at how relieved I feel and at how much I want things to be okay between us. My brain wants to believe it's just as friends, but the *petit allegro* my heart is performing inside my chest hints that it may be more than that. "We're even," I say.

"Good." He turns to go but then stops. "I haven't had dinner yet. Would you be up for a burger? I was thinking of going across the street to the diner."

I've already eaten, but I have a sudden craving for a chocolate shake. Or at least I tell myself that's what I'm craving. "Sure. Sounds great."

He steps to the side and makes a sweeping motion toward the door. "After you."

Chapter
TWENTY-THREE

The Leesburg Diner is an old-fashioned place with black-and-white checkered floors, silver stools surrounding a counter, about a dozen cozy booths and tables, and a coin-operated jukebox. It also has the best milkshakes in all of Loudoun County.

"Seat yourself," the woman at the counter calls to us as we walk in.

"Your choice," Darius says.

I feel torn. A booth is more private, but the counter seems more fun, more romantic. *Did I seriously just think that?* I clear my throat and point to a table—the most non-private, unromantic table in the room. "This seems good."

The restaurant is half empty, so we place our orders quickly. "So, is Jaycee your only sibling?" I ask as our waitress shuffles away.

Darius shakes his head. "We have a half-sister, Ellie. She's four. She and Jaycee both live with my mom and stepdad in Fairfax. I'm in Sterling with my dad."

"Oh. Is that because of … your transfer?"

He nods but doesn't elaborate. "How about you? Any brothers or sisters?"

I tell him all about Andrew and how he takes after my parents while I … don't. "Art is totally not my thing." I want to add *and I can't believe it's yours*, but that might lead to a discussion of a certain computerized love match. I'm not ready to go there, even though I may be getting used to the idea that Darius is not a total loser and does, in fact, have a certain charm about him. Not to mention he has eyes I could lose myself in and brown bangs I kind of want to run my fingers through and … OMIGOSH WHAT IS WRONG WITH ME?

"Shake?" Our waitress slams a glass down, bringing me back to reality.

I take a deep breath "Thank you." I busy myself with my straw, poking at the mountain of whipped cream. I refuse to lift my head for fear that my eyes somehow may betray the fact that moments ago I was daydreaming about caressing Darius's curls.

"Hey. Are you okay?" He grabs my free hand in his, and I pull it away as though his touch has scorched me.

"What? Yes. What are you—"

He looks at me with a mixture of concern and amusement. "Easy, easy. I just meant … " He gently touches my palm, sending a shiver up my arm.

Ah. *The cuts.* Which are really more like pokes and are so tiny, I'm not sure how he even noticed. My face burns as I realize I've way overreacted to his touch. "Those are nothing. An unfortunate encounter with a compass." He raises his eyebrows in apparent disbelief, so I add, "Not the direction-telling kind; the circle-drawing kind."

"Right. I figured that part out." He leans forward and rests his arms on the table. "Sorry to make you jump. Did you seriously think I was making a move on you? Because I want you to know, I'm much smoother than that. You'll barely see it coming when I make my move."

My stomach suddenly feels as though all sixteen of Ms. DuBois's Tip Toe Toddlers are flitting around in it. Still, I force myself to stay calm and meet his gaze. "Is that so?"

"Trust me. Smooth."

The waitress reappears with his burger in hand, placing it on the table.

"That looks yummy."

He points to my shake as he prepares to take his first bite. "So does that."

"I love their shakes. Super creamy." I pluck the maraschino cherry from top. "Want my cherry?"

Darius's eyes widen, and he chokes on his burger. He grabs a fistful of napkins and holds them to his mouth.

Meanwhile, my face turns what I can only assume is a shade redder than the offending fruit in my hand. "Oh, wow. I mean ... I didn't ... I just meant I don't like these. Holy crap, are you okay?"

He's still coughing, but he nods. I can't help but giggle, and soon we're both laughing so hard everyone in the restaurant is staring at us.

When I finally recover, I lean back in my chair and pull

a straight face. "What was it you were just saying? Oh, right, how smooth you are. How could I forget?"

He mock-scowls, grabs the cherry from my hand, and pops it into his mouth, sending me into another round of giggles.

"I like your laugh," he says. "It's sweet."

I take a long draw of my milkshake, hoping it will cool down the burn on my cheeks. *Your laugh is sweet?* Who says things like that? Who is this boy?

He holds up one finger. "Be right back." He stands and walks over to the jukebox. It has a mix of songs from the fifties and today's pop. He turns and grins at me as he makes his selection, and a vaguely familiar oldie comes on with a round of ooh-wahs, followed by the first line: "Earth angel, earth angel."

"Cute," I call as he walks back toward me.

"And smooth."

"Pretty smooth."

He hesitates when he reaches the table, and for a moment I fear he's going to ask me to dance because that seems like the kind of thing he might do just to embarrass me, but he flips his chair around backward and sits down, straddling it. He must have noticed me eyeing his fries earlier, because he picks one up and offers it to me. I don't say no. Leesburg Diner's fries are almost as good as their shakes.

"Where did you learn to write rap?" I ask.

"YouTube."

"Who's your favorite artist?"

He grimaces. "None of them. I hate rap. I'm more of a Johnny Cash kind of guy."

"Sooo … you watch rap videos as a form of self-torture?"

He laughs. "I don't watch rap videos." He offers me another fry. "I wanted to do a song for our project, but I'm not exactly Pavarotti. I figured maybe I could pull off a rap, so I went onto YouTube and searched for 'learn how to write a rap song.'"

"Are you serious?"

"Yeah. There's this dude on there with a whole series of lessons. He's really good. At rap and at teaching it."

"He must be."

Darius's eyes shine. "Because it was sick, right? And you liked it."

"You're not going to let it rest until I admit that I liked it, are you?"

"Can I consider that your admission?"

I roll my eyes. "You can. Congratulations. It was a great rap."

"Yes." He pumps his fist on the table. "Now. What about the dancing? Did you like my dancing?"

I purse my lips and point my straw at him. "Don't push it."

But I can tell by his grin that he sees past my front. Because I did like his dancing. I liked it very much.

Chapter
TWENTY-FOUR

I slam my laptop shut, toss it to the foot of my bed, and sink back into my pillow. College application essays are the worst, especially when you're trying to explain to MIT's dean of admissions how you've developed a complex computer algorithm with an error rate of an almost negligible 2.9 percent, despite the fact that it is aimed at calculating one of the most incalculable things in the world—the human heart.

I stare at my faux stucco ceiling and pick out the designs in the bumps and swirls. There's an eagle's wing and a raccoon, and—when I squint a bit—a lopsided star. I stare at it, searching for answers.

I have been enamored with Ty since the first day of ninth grade, when he walked into advanced algebra and flashed that perfect smile at me on the way to his desk. Even then, he seemed so sure of himself and his place in the world, despite the fact that we were two of the only freshmen in a class made up of mostly sophomores. That kind of swagger was something I'd never had a day in my life, and I envied it. I wanted it. Not just in a boyfriend, but for myself.

And with Ty, I got it. I became a braver, stronger version of me. I'd give anything to get that back, but what if I never do? Maybe it's time to admit that it's over between us and, despite what he said six months ago, this is a perma-break. And, maybe, as much as it pains me to think about it, Ty and I were never meant to be. After all, Libby is close to perfect, and she says he's not my match.

Which brings me to … Darius. I pull my pillow over my face. I'm afraid to admit it even to a lopsided star, but for some crazy, inconceivable reason, I can't help but smile when I think of Darius Groves. My heart did an undeniable flip tonight when he appeared in front of me and called me "Bright Angel." And when he asked me to go to the diner. And when he told me I had a sweet laugh, and when he put on "Earth Angel" and, and, and … I squeeze my pillow and slam it against the wall. "Aaaaarrrgh!"

I grab my phone. I want to text him. Or more accurately, I want to text him so he'll text me back so I can see his name on my screen and imagine his voice in my head. I type in the first thought that comes to mind.

```
Alicea: Johnny Cash? That's pretty old
school.
```

I stare at my phone. Nothing. No text, no typing bubble, nothing. This was a bad idea. What was I thinking? He's probably staring at his cell right now wondering why I'm stalking him. I'm losing my mind, all because of a silly rap song and some flirting. And no doubt the flirting is merely his way of getting under my skin. He's messing with me because of our match.

I toss my phone onto my desk and head across the hall to the bathroom. A minute later, my mouth full of toothpaste, I hear my phone ding. I practically mow Andrew down in the hallway as I fly back to my room.

"What the—"

I slam my door on him, then realize I seriously need to spit out my toothpaste, so I rush back to the bathroom past a dubious Andrew, rinse, and run back to my phone.

```
Darius: It's the rebel in me.
Darius: What kind of stuff do you like?
```

I smile and press my phone to my cheek.

```
Alicea: Normal stuff.
Alicea: Taylor. Rihanna. Adele.
Alicea: Guess I'm not much of a rebel.
Darius: What's the most rebellious thing
you've ever done?
```

Besides text with a boy who got expelled from his last school? I close my eyes. What the heck am I doing?

```
Alicea: I went vegetarian for four days a
few years ago.
```

```
Darius: What happened?
Alicea. I didn't eat meat.
Darius: Yeah, I figured that part. But why
did you quit?
Alicea: Oh, hahaha. Sorry.
Alicea: Andrew brought home a meat-lovers
from Italiano's.
Darius: Ouch. That'll stamp out the rebel
in anybody.
Alicea: It was delicious. I have no regrets.
Alicea: What about you?
Darius: Nope. I've never gone vegetarian.
Alicea: Haha. I meant, what's the most
rebellious thing you've ever done?
```

I watch as he types and types and types, but he must go back and delete it all, because his answer is three short words.

```
Darius: Who, me? Nothing.
Alicea: Right.
Darius: C U 2morrow, Bright Angel.
Alicea: :P
Alicea: Good night.
```

I lie down, but it takes me a long time to fall asleep. Partly because I can't wait to see Darius tomorrow. And partly because I have no idea how I should act when I do.

Chapter TWENTY-FIVE

"If I tell you, you have to swear not to tell anyone. Not even Brie. Not yet."

Maggs shuts her locker door and leans back on it. "Of course."

I glance around to make sure no one is within earshot. My entire being cringes as I squeeze my eyes shut and blurt it out. "I think I like Darius Groves."

There. I've said it out loud and to another person and it didn't kill me.

I revel in a brief sense of relief, until I open my eyes and see Maggs's incredulous expression.

"For real?" she asks.

"Crap. I know. It's crazy, right? I mean, to go from Ty to him. What am I thinking? This is stupid on so many levels. Forget I even said anything. It's some sort of temporary insan—"

Maggs grabs my arms. "Alicea, stop. I was surprised, that's all. It's not stupid or insane. You're allowed to like whoever you want."

I blink, and for a moment, the world stops.

I'm allowed to like whoever I want.

Maggs makes it sound so simple. And for her, I'm sure it is. For me? Not so much. Darius is outside my lines. He's flawed and messy and makes me uncomfortable.

But maybe I'm allowed to like him anyway.

"Why can't we tell Brie?" Maggs asks. "She'll be psyched."

"I know, but that's exactly why I don't want to say anything. I can't handle her enthusiasm yet. I need to take this slow. We'll tell her soon, I promise."

Maggs smiles. "Okay. I get that."

As we turn to walk toward our homerooms, I assume what I hope is an innocent tone. "Speaking of liking whoever we want, who are you into these days? Anyone in particular?"

She shrugs. "Not really. You know. Everyone. No one."

"So nobody specific? Are you sure?"

"Pretty sure."

I sigh. "How do you do that?"

"Do what?"

"Not care about who you like and who likes you. I wish I could not care."

"It's not that I don't care. I guess I just don't … worry."

"Of course you don't. You're Maggs."

She stops walking and her eyes narrow. "What's that supposed to mean?"

"Nothing. You're Sugar Magnolia, that's all. Like the song says, you're 'going where the wind goes.' Sometimes I wish I could be like that."

"It's not always easy being me, you know."

I nod. "Okay."

"I know what people say about me, but it's not like I *want* to be that girl. Trust me, if I could be like you, I would. I'd give anything to be so sure of myself."

Me? Sure of myself? She has to be kidding. "Maggs, I'm the least sure-of-myself person I know."

"Well, you're sure of who you like. Or at least, you were until now." As the bell rings, she gives me a teasing grin and walks backward away from me. "I know who Alicea likes," she sings.

I stick out my tongue. "Not a word. To anyone."

During my first period class, I screw up a simple computer code, causing my team's program to conclude that the odds of rolling five ones in a single Yahtzee roll is one-in-three, and during second period I spill water all over my physics lab table while trying to test Archimedes's principle. By the time I get to third-period lunch, I'm such a mess I can't eat. Next period is study hall with Darius, and I'm equal parts nervous and excited.

When fourth period finally arrives, I find him sitting alone in the same carrel where we first met to start our lit project. He glances up as I approach him, a slow smile spreading across his face. "Hey, Bright Angel. Or do you still not want me to call you that?"

I sit down next to him. "What's in a name? That which we call an angel by any other name would be as bright."

His smile widens, and his eyebrows dance. "I love it when you talk Elizabethan to me."

I feel myself blushing, so I turn and busy myself with extracting my calculus book from my backpack.

"Do you know what this Friday is?" Darius asks me as I flip through to find my lesson.

I shake my head.

"The next girls' home game. And I believe you have a certain promise to keep to a certain little sister who basically asks me every single day when she's going to meet her idol."

"I will be there," I say. "And I will not let that certain little sister down."

"Cool. That'll be … I mean, she'll be really excited."

I nod. "Should be fun."

"Do you have a way to get there? To the game? Because I could pick you up if you need a ride."

I hesitate, my eyes glued to my calc problems, and Darius leans closer. "It's not that I don't trust you to be there, it's just I can't take another week of her bugging me."

I turn and look into his eyes. Is he trying to turn this into a date? I mean, a date with his kid sister along, but still.

I don't need a ride, but I find myself nodding and saying "sure, thanks" and typing my address into his phone.

And, just like that, I—*omigosh*—have an almost, sort of, pseudo date with Darius Groves and his kid sister.

Chapter
TWENTY-SIX

At Friday afternoon's all-school pep rally, I steer Maggs and Brie to our usual seats next to the section where the soccer team always sits. Only this time, it's not for me, it's for Maggs.

Brie shakes her head at me as we sit down, and I'm tempted to explain, but I keep my mouth shut. She's having dinner tonight with some relatives and won't be at the basketball game, so I should be able to keep the whole Darius Groves thing—whatever it is—a secret from her for at least one more weekend. Let her think I'm still chasing Ty.

"This is awesome." Maggs is bouncing up and down in her seat, her eyes bright. She loves pep rallies. "Are we ready to get loud?"

"Oh, yeah," I say. "Go, Pats, go."

"Woo. Hoo." Brie echoes my sarcastic tone, but Maggs appears not to notice.

She holds up her fist for a bump. "We are the Patriots of Grand View High. Victory, victory is our cry!"

I laugh. "Maggs, Maggs, Maggs. If you weren't so hippified, I swear you'd have been a cheerleader."

"And what's so wrong with that? For your information, I almost did try out freshman year, but then I remembered I don't do short skirts." She points at the squad lined up at the far end of the court. "Pompoms, on the other hand. Those are the bomb."

As the last few members of the senior class file into the bleachers, Principal Cho taps a microphone at center court. "Welcome, Grand View students and faculty! How are you this Friday afternoon?" With the exception of the cheerleaders, a few teachers, and—of course—Maggs, the response is tepid, prompting him to repeat: "I said, how are you this Friday afternoooooon?"

This time we oblige with applause and some hooting, and Cho officially kicks off the rally. He calls in the girls' and boys' volleyball teams and tennis teams, then the soccer teams. Ty runs in, pumping his fist in the air and shouting. I can't help but watch him as he crosses the court. It's a habit, as natural as breathing, and my heart twists a bit inside my chest as he stops, searches the stands, and points at Becca, awarding her with his dazzling smile before taking his seat with the team.

I catch Aiden's attention and motion for him to sit near us. He grins and manages to squeeze past a couple of his teammates, ending up right next to Maggs.

Next is the main event—the boys' and girls' basketball teams. As they enter the gym, Lexi and her boyfriend—Chris

Broder, the star of our boys' team—spar off under the far basket in a mock game of one-on-one. When Chris finally grabs her and lifts her in the air for a dunk, the crowd erupts in cheers.

"They're adorable," Maggs shouts into my ear.

I grin and nod. Pep rallies aren't my thing, but I have to agree with her. Chris and Lexi are total relationship goals.

As the cheerleaders take the floor and start their dance routine to "Hey, Ya," I catch Abi's eye. She's stationed in front of us, and she gives me a slight nod. I take a deep breath. Cool. My plan is on.

The song ends, and Abi grabs a megaphone. "I need two volunteers," she shouts. "Who's willing to come down here and show their Grand View spirit?"

Maggs jumps up and down, hand raised, because of course she does. Abi grins and heads up the bleachers toward us. "Maggie Maloney," she shouts. "Thank you." She looks around, ignoring all the boys whose hands have suddenly shot up, and her gaze settles on Aiden. "And what about you? Want to join the fun?"

Aiden looks startled, but he nods and follows Abi and Maggs down the steps.

Abi points them to center court, then heads over to the basketball players' section and grabs Lexi and Chris. She drags them out to join Maggs and Aiden.

"Is everyone ready for this?" she shouts.

A cheer rises up, though no one seems quite sure what's about to happen, least of all her four victims. "We're going to play a little game of two-on-two," she says. "Maggie and Aiden versus Lexi and Chris."

Maggs and Lexi laugh and give each other high-fives, while Aiden and Chris spar off with some obvious trash talking. Principal Cho tosses Chris a basketball, sending him and Lexi charging down the court. They pass the ball back and forth, weaving it in and out between their legs and behind their backs while Aiden and Maggs follow after them, laughing and occasionally swatting in the general direction of the ball. Lexi stops at the edge of the court and spins it on her finger, just out of Aiden's reach, before tossing it to Chris for a perfect alley-oop.

Next, Aiden takes the ball out and inbounds it to Maggs, who attempts to dribble. Lexi and Chris run circles around her, pretending to try to steal the ball as she wobbles her way down the court. About halfway down, she bounces the ball to Aiden, who takes it the rest of the way toward the basket. As Maggs joins him, he tosses it back and signals for her to shoot. She shakes her head, but he insists. Maggs tosses the ball up, missing the net by a mile, but Aiden jumps up and tips it so it glances off the backboard and into the basket.

The four of them and the entire gym erupt into cheers, and Maggs launches herself into Aiden's arms for a hug. They dance around a bit before heading back toward our spot in the bleachers.

Brie turns to me, grins, and holds her hand up for a high five. "For someone who insists she doesn't like to get involved in boyfriend whispering, you're pretty good at it."

I grin. "Victory, victory is our cry."

Chapter
TWENTY-SEVEN

The front passenger-side door of Darius's blue Camry is … not blue. It's yellow. He apologizes as he opens it for me, explaining that he plans to get it painted to match the rest of the car as soon as he saves up enough money. I smile and assure him it's fine, and though I can't help but briefly compare his car with a certain tricked-out BMW coupe, it *is* fine.

As I settle into my seat, I turn toward his sister, who is practically bouncing up and down in the back. "You ready to meet Lexi?"

She nods, her eyes shining. "I brought a Sharpie and this article for her to sign. Does that seem stupid?" She holds up a *Loudoun Times* piece that ran last month about Lexi signing to play for the College of William and Mary. The school is not exactly a basketball powerhouse, but it does have a good business entrepreneurship program. Apparently Lexi decided that was more important to her than basketball.

"That doesn't seem stupid at all," I answer. "I bet she'll love to sign it for you."

"What did you think about that?" Darius asks. "William and Mary—smart decision or waste of talent?"

I shrug. "I was shocked, obviously." Everyone was. Lexi could have gone anywhere. Even UConn, the best women's basketball program in the country, was recruiting her. "I don't get it. When you're that good at something … to throw it away like that. It seems crazy."

"Yeah, but look at her." Darius points to the photo, where Lexi is smiling as though she's won the lottery.

"I know, but don't you think … " I sigh, not entirely sure what to think myself. "She could be living the dream. I mean, come on. She has a nine-year-old asking for her autograph."

"Ten," Jaycee interjects.

"I'm sorry. Ten. Why would you turn your back on that?"

Darius pushes his bangs off his forehead, and his eyes meet mine. "Sometimes what seems right to everyone else and what's actually right are two different things. People act like Lexi owed it to the world to play for UConn. But this is her life, her call. I think she's brave."

"Brave," I repeat. From what I'd heard, her parents weren't exactly thrilled with her decision. Neither was her coach. "That's one word for it."

"One thing's for sure." Jaycee looks back and forth at her brother and me. "She'll start as a freshman."

I laugh. "True that."

We're playing the Potomac Run Panthers, one of the worst teams in the county, so the game is a rout, with Grand View up by twenty points in the fourth quarter.

"You should have tried out for our guys' team," I tell Darius as the last few minutes tick away. It's clear from his play-by-play commentary to Jaycee that he knows the sport inside and out. "I bet you would have made it. And they need all the help they can get. They haven't been very good the past few years."

Darius shrugs. "I don't play sports. I watch."

I sneak a glance at him. Why doesn't he play? He certainly has the build of an athlete.

"He used to be a guard," Jaycee pipes in. "He was good, too."

Darius nudges her. "Yeah, well. 'Used to be' is the key phrase."

"Why'd you quit?"

"Long story."

"He didn't quit, he—"

Darius nudges her again, hard. "Yo, did you see that?" He points toward the far end of the court. "Number eighteen tripped Lexi for no reason. Hey, ref!"

Half the crowd is now standing and shouting. Darius avoids my gaze as I try to fill in the blanks. I'm guessing he got tossed off the team, for fighting or mouthing off at his coach or maybe even drugs. *What in the world am I doing? Sure, Darius is a good dancer and has those deep blue eyes and likes my laugh and calls me "Angel" and makes my brain all melty, but clearly he has issues. The last thing I need is a boy with issues.*

When the buzzer finally sounds, I stand and hold up my hand for Jaycee. "Ready to do this?"

She gives me a high-five, her eyes wide and bright. "I am so ready."

"Have fun," Darius says. "I'll wait here."

Jaycee follows me down the steps, clutching the Sharpie and the newspaper article to her chest. The crowd has started to swarm the team. I spot Lexi holding hands with Chris near mid-court, and by the time we reach them, the floor is packed.

"Hey, Lexi. I have someone I'd like you to meet."

Lexi and Chris both turn. Little Miss Chatterbox holds out her pen and the article, her mouth agape, star-struck and wordless. *So* adorable.

Lexi squeals. "You want my autograph? Cool! I feel so big-time." She laughs and tells Chris to turn around so she can lean on his back to write.

Chris starts to pivot, but then turns back to her. "Is that thing going to bleed through to my shirt?"

Lexi shrugs. "Worst-case scenario, it does and you have my autograph on the back of your shirt."

"Good point." Chris laughs and gives her a quick kiss before turning back around.

I sigh. Those two have what everyone wants. What I want, and what I once had with Ty. Could I ever have that with someone like Darius? I honestly don't—

"Hey, watch it!"

All of a sudden, seemingly out of nowhere, Lexi is sprawled on the gym floor with number eighteen from the other team standing over her shouting. What the—? Chris turns around, clearly shocked, but as he tries to help Lexi up, he's knocked down beside her by a crowd of Lexi's teammates rushing toward her aggressor.

The next thing I know, players, students, and even a few parents are pushing and kicking and throwing punches. A bunch of cell phones come out as people try to record the melee. As I retreat from the hostile crowd, I reach out to grab Jaycee's hand. Only she's not there. Where did she go?

"Jaycee!" My shout barely registers among the stomps and hollers of what has quickly become a mob. I twist left and right, frantically searching the crowd. I have to get her out of here. This is no place for a—"Whoa!" A huge guy in a Panthers letter jacket pushes me on his way to the middle of the action, and I step hard on the foot of a girl with dreads.

"Careful!" She grabs my arm, her eyes blazing.

"Sorry. He pushed me." I back up, and she lets go with a sneer. I narrowly avoid getting knocked around again as two girls who can't possibly be older than freshmen go at it, pulling each other's hair and throwing punches.

One of the referees rushes in, blowing her whistle and shouting for everyone to stop, but this is not a game, and no one listens. Someone slams into my shoulder, and a flash of pain shoots up my neck. I spot a guy a few feet away with a stream of blood pouring from his nose. Black spots circle before my eyes, and my head feels light. I can't get enough air. I squeeze through the crowd to courtside and collapse to my knees, my head in my hands.

Chapter
TWENTY-EIGHT

"Alicea. Are you okay?" Darius's voice sounds as faint as an echo, but it's enough to help clear the cobwebs.

I peer up at him and take a deep breath, the pain in my neck still sharp. "I'm fine. Did you see which way Jaycee went?"

"I grabbed her."

It's then that I notice his sister standing behind him, tears in her eyes, clutching her signed article. "Are you okay?" I ask.

She nods.

"I need to get her out of here," Darius says.

"Of course." I stand up, trying to appear as though I'm fine, but Darius notices as I wince.

"You're hurt."

"It's no big deal." I nod toward the still-growing mob at center court. "Let's go."

We pass four sheriff's deputies on our way down the hall. "This is insane. I can't believe that b—" I look down at Jaycee and opt not to finish my thought. Instead, I feign a bright tone. "Well, that was an exciting way to get an autograph, wasn't it?"

She nods. "Just as Lexi handed it back to me, that girl knocked her down. Do you think she's okay?"

"I'm sure she will be. Lexi's tough. And her whole team was right there to help."

Darius and I exchange glances. "How about we get some sundaes at Friendly's on the way home?" he asks her. "We'll go through the drive-through."

Jaycee beams. "That'll work."

"Sundaes for everyone, then." He turns to me, his expression guarded. "Do you mind if I drive her to our mom's first and then bring you home?"

I blink. I get the feeling he's trying to turn the end of this bizarre night into an almost, sort of, pseudo, sister-less date.

"Sure, whatever's easiest," I say. Because apparently I am going to let him.

I check my social media as we drive. It appears the cops broke up the fighting soon after they arrived. A couple of Potomac Run students were arrested, and one of our players went to the hospital with minor injuries. No news on Lexi, so I assume she made it out in one piece.

The sundaes are amazing. Darius, of course, charms the server into putting extra caramel on his sister's. When we get to their mom's house, he bomps her forehead, and we watch as she lets herself into the house.

"She's so sweet," I say. "I wish I had sisters."

"She's sweet when she wants to be." He turns and grins. "Thanks for coming tonight. And for taking her to meet Lexi."

"Of course. A promise is a promise."

As we drive toward my house, I lean my head back into the seat and close my eyes, exhausted as the events of the night catch up with me. I don't even realize I'm rubbing my neck until Darius points it out.

"You should probably put some ice on that," he says.

I drop my hands to my lap. "I'll be fine. Seriously."

He scowls. "I'm so sorry you ended up in the middle of that mob. And I'm sorry I didn't get you out right away. I was just so focused on Jaycee that I—"

"It's fine. You did the right thing. She's so little, she could have really gotten hurt. But how did you get there so quickly?"

"I saw number eighteen heading toward Lexi and figured something might go down. I was only a few feet away when she pushed her."

I steal a glance at his profile as he drives. A small scar snakes along his right jawline, and his usually playful, irreverent expression is replaced by an intensity I'm not used to seeing. How did he get the scar? I'm not sure I want to know, though I must admit, I do kind of like the protective streak. "You really watch out for your sister, don't you?"

"She's been through a lot." He doesn't elaborate. He never elaborates, so I decide to push.

"You mean, because of your parents' divorce?"

He shakes his head. "No. She was so little when that happened, she doesn't really remember."

We pull onto my street, but Darius stops a few houses away and cuts the engine and the headlights.

Are we … parking? Is he going to try to kiss me?

I bite the inside of my lip, suddenly unsure of what to do with my hands, what to say, or where to look.

"The thing is … Jaycee doesn't have a lot of friends," he says.

"What? Why not? She's so smart and sweet and—"

"I know. It's stupid, but … sometimes she has seizures. They're pretty freaky, and you know kids. So mean."

"Seizures? You mean, like epilepsy?"

He shrugs. "Sort of. It's not epilepsy, but the doctors aren't sure what it is. They're super random. We never know when they'll happen."

"Wow. Poor kid. That must be scary."

"Basketball is the one thing that makes her happy," he says. "She's good at it. Really good. Tonight meant a lot to her."

I smile at him. "I'm glad I was able to help. And I'm glad you were there to get her out of that mess when you did."

He nods. "Me too. Are you sure your neck is going to be—"

"Totally. It's fine."

Darius says nothing for a long minute. He sinks back into his seat and stares out the windshield. With each passing second, I find myself feeling less and less nervous about the prospect of kissing him, and more and more worried that he might take me home *without* trying to kiss me.

Finally, without a word, he starts the engine back up and drives toward my house. *Shoot. Should I have said something, or ... done something? Moved closer to him?*

As he pulls up to the curb by our driveway, he turns, and our eyes meet.

"Thanks again."

"Sure. You're a great brother, you know that?"

"And you are a true Angel Bright."

I feel myself blushing. I'm not sure anyone has ever paid me a nicer compliment. It's almost as nice as a kiss. Almost.

Chapter

TWENTY-NINE

Dewdrop? I blink as I study the list outside Ms. DuBois's office. Danica Morris has been cast as the Snow Queen and Monique Brown as the Sugar Plum Fairy in our dance school's annual performance of *The Nutcracker*. No surprises there. But me? The lead for the "Waltz of the Flowers"?

"Oh my gosh, Alicea!" Maggs tackles me from behind.

"Ow, ow, ow." I clutch the back of my neck. It's much better than the other night. It's healing, thanks to Darius's suggestion of continuing to ice it, but it definitely cannot withstand a Maggs Maloney tackle.

"Sorry," Maggs says. "But, a solo! How amazing is that?"

It's pretty freaking amazing. Each year, our studio performs a few pieces from the *Nutcracker* Suite at the Leesburg First Night Celebration, a huge New Year's Eve event where local artists and musicians perform at shops and restaurants throughout town. At midnight, the activities end and everyone gathers on the courthouse lawn to light candles and ring in the New Year.

"You're going to be fabulous. And you get to wear the Dewdrop tiara. I am so, so, so jealous." Maggs is jumping up and down, so great is her enthusiasm for my role.

"Thanks. I guess." My eyes remain trained on the list.

"What do you mean, 'I guess'?"

"I don't know. Dewdrop seems so … not me." Dewdrop is a fairy. She's light and airy and free. She flutters. I may perform a *jete* like a boss, but fluttering is not my specialty. Ms. DuBois is forever urging me to work on my *vivacité*.

"Are you crazy? Dewdrop is totally—"

"Ladies." Ms. DuBois appears at Maggs's side.

I straighten and smile and generally try to give the appearance of someone whose neck isn't throbbing. Surely it will heal up over the next few weeks. I can fake it until then. Can't I?

"Hello, Ms. DuBois." Maggs squeezes my arm. "Great choice for Dewdrop. This girl's going to kill it."

Ms. DuBois offers a slight nod in my direction. "I have no doubt." And with that, she disappears into her office.

"See?" Maggs says. "She thinks Dewdrop is you."

"I don't know. Maybe she—"

"Congrats." Brie walks by, barely pausing to acknowledge us as she heads into the studio.

Maggs and I exchange a look. "What was that about?" she asks.

"No idea." I walk to the door and peer through the window at Brie as she stretches in front of the mirror. "Do you think she wanted Dewdrop?" Brie has never been competitive about dance roles, but maybe she has tiara envy, too.

Maggs shakes her head. "I doubt it. She knows she's not that good."

"Maggs!"

She laughs. "Just saying. No offense to Brie. I'm not that good, either. She and I will make awesome flowers."

I debate whether to go in and ask Brie what's wrong, but before I can decide, Ms. DuBois emerges, clapping, from her office. "Let's go, ladies. We have a lot of work to do and only five weeks to do it."

I spend half the class trying not to show any signs of pain. Luckily, Ms. DuBois starts us off with a simple walk-through of the choreography, so the strain on my neck is minimal. I spend the other half worrying about Brie, who goes out of her way to avoid eye contact with me. At one point, Ms. DuBois sets us in front of each other, face-to-face. We are stuck that way for a solid two minutes as she positions each of our classmates, but Brie stares at the floor the entire time, her expression dark.

Shoot. She is jealous, I know it. We sat next to each other this morning in physics class and she was perfectly fine. She even listened to me rattle on about the latest season of *Stranger Things*, though I know for a fact she hates the show.

As the hour wraps up and we head to the dressing room, I stop Maggs. "Brie's definitely mad at me about something. She was weird the whole class."

"Tell me about it. I felt awkward just being in the same room with you two."

"Think she'll go to the Juice Joint with us?"

"I hope so. I'm dying to know what her problem—" But before Maggs can finish her sentence, Brie rushes out of the dressing room, her jeans pulled on over her leotard and her sneakers barely laced, heading toward the door.

"Brie!" Maggs shouts to her, but while she stops, she doesn't turn around. "We're heading over for smoothies. Aren't you coming?"

I hold my breath. Brie hesitates, still facing the door. "Are you sure you want me to?"

"What? Of course we do."

"Really?" She turns and glares, her hands balled in fists at her side. "Because I'm sure you two have things you want to talk about—secrets that for whatever reason you've decided not to share with someone who is supposed to be your best friend."

"What? What are you … ?" I stop and suck in my breath as the realization strikes. *Darius. She knows.* "Brie. We weren't keeping secrets. We were planning to—"

"You lied to me." She takes a step forward. Girls are streaming out of the dressing room and staring at us as they walk by, but Brie seems not to notice. "You told me you were going to the game with your parents. But this afternoon, during world history, a bunch of us were watching a video of the brawl, and there you were walking out of the gym holding hands with a guy who supposedly you want nothing to do with."

"We weren't holding hands." My cheeks grow warm, though I'm not sure whether it's because I'm embarrassed that Brie caught me in the lie or because my heart has started pounding at the thought of holding hands with Darius.

"But you were with him. And not your parents." Brie's voice wavers as she turns to Maggs. "And I'm sure you knew all about it."

"Maggs wanted to tell you," I say. "And I swear, I was about to."

"Whatever." Brie dismisses us with a wave of her hand. "I'm over it." She turns to leave, slamming the door with a bang that makes it clear she most certainly is not over it.

I trudge into the dressing room and slump onto a bench. This sucks. I kept my pseudo date with Darius a secret from Brie because I wanted to avoid her drama. Talk about a plan backfiring.

Chapter THIRTY

I'm not sure if it's all in my imagination or if things have gotten awkward, but the past two days have been a bit weird with Darius. He did ask me about my neck Monday morning, and we've smiled at each other a few times in class, but that's been it. So I'm nervous as I walk into study hall Tuesday afternoon.

I spot his curls above the back carrel and have to fight the urge to grab a desk up front. As I walk toward him, so many thoughts swirl in my head. Why didn't he kiss me Friday night? Did he even think of our outing as a pseudo date? Maybe he really was just trying to help his sister get Lexi's autograph, and maybe he dropped her off first because he wanted to get her home early for bed. Worse, maybe he did think of the whole thing as a date but decided by the end that he had no desire to kiss me.

Or maybe this whole stupid thing is in my head. Well, and in Libby's almost infallible program.

"Hey." I tap his shoulder.

He looks up, and his smile chases away all my worries. He simultaneously pulls out his ear bud and the chair next to him so I can sit down. "Hello, Angel Bright."

I can't help but grin. I sit and nod toward his notebook. "What are you working on?"

"A report."

"Duh. For what?"

Darius leans toward me. "*Español.*"

"Can you read it to me?" I don't know a word of Spanish, but I like the thought of Darius speaking it to me.

"Sorry," he says. "*No está listo.*"

"What? *No hablo español.*"

He laughs. "It's a work in progress."

"That's okay. I want to hear what you have so far."

He shakes his head. "Maybe when it's done."

"Mmhmm. Correct me if I'm wrong, but isn't that what you said about your mixed media project?"

His eyebrows shoot up. He is clearly surprised that I remember. "So I did. And so I will. When it's done."

"Right." I purse my lips.

"Hey." His eyes hold mine. "I mean it."

"Promise?"

"Promise."

I hold out my pinkie. I haven't done a pinkie promise since I was, like, eight. I'm not sure if I'm regressing or if this is just an excuse to touch Darius's hand.

Darius's eyes never leave mine as he takes my pinkie in

his. "Pinkie promise," he says.

"Okay, then." I start to pull away, but he tightens his grip and draws my hand in closer toward him, slowly, closer and closer until it is inches from his lips. I hold my breath as he ducks his head, eyes still trained on mine, and kisses my pinkie nail.

Whoa. That was … unexpected. And despite the fact that it was my fingernail and not my lips or my throat or my earlobe or even my cheek, it was one of the most sensual kisses I've ever had. I have a serious urge to lean over and kiss his lips—long and hard—but the looming presence of twenty-six of our classmates, not to mention our study hall monitor, keeps me from doing it.

Instead, I tear a piece of paper from his notebook and write on it: *F Hall janitor's closet*. And then I ask Ms. Glendon for a pass to the library to check out some reference materials.

Chapter
THIRTY-ONE

The closet smells like lemons, and I breathe it in. It's dark. I consider turning on the light, but I don't. I need it dark to calm my nerves.

What am I doing? Meeting a boy—any boy, much less Darius Groves—in the janitor's closet is a highly un-Alicea-Springer-like move.

That pinkie-nail kiss was *so* hot, though.

I bite my lip, hard, and give myself a pep talk: *Calm down, Alicea. You'll do fine. Remember? Kissing a boy is as normal and natural and simple as breathing.*

At last the door creaks open, and Darius stands in front of me, silhouetted by the hallway light. I can't see his expression, but I can feel his smile.

I pull the door closed and grab his hand. He takes a small step toward me. The smell of lemons is replaced with his woodsy scent as his lips touch mine.

His lips are soft, and though his kiss is light and tentative, his free hand wraps around my lower back and draws me close. I press myself into him, and just like that, our kiss goes from sweet to smoky.

He backs me into the closet wall. A mop handle lodges itself into my shoulder blade, but I barely feel it. My senses are overwhelmed with his mouth, his hands, and the sensation of my fingers tangled in his soft curls. *Curls are definitely my new favorite thing.* I gasp as his lips move downward to kiss my chin and throat to a space right under my left ear that I'd never realized was so sensitive.

"I've wanted to do this for a long time," he murmurs.

"Mmhmm." It's all I can manage. I instruct my brain not to wonder what constitutes a "long time." Overthinking does not pair well with class-cutting dark-closet kissing.

And then, as his lips make their way back up to mine, I become incapable of even a single thought. I am only skin, and tingling nerves, and mouth, and deep breaths. My head and my body feel a-jumble—dazed and disheveled and scattered—everything I'm not—but it feels like the only thing I've ever really wanted.

Until he pulls away. "I should go."

My eyes widen, and I shake my head. "What? No."

"I know. I'm sorry." He holds up a bathroom pass. "It was the best I could do."

"A bathroom pass? Really?" My tone is light, teasing, though my disappointment is real.

He kisses the tip of my nose in an apology. "You'd already asked for the library pass. I didn't want to raise suspicions."

I pull him back for one more kiss and then another before he opens the closet door and disappears with a wink and a smile.

I crouch down against the wall, blinking and shaking my head to clear the fog. I spend the rest of the class period sitting in the dark closet, breathing in the lemon scent and steadying my heart rate.

Wow. That was wild and exciting and insane. And it was nothing at all like breathing.

Chapter
THIRTY-TWO

Thanksgiving is quiet, as is typical at the Springer household. All of our relatives live on the West Coast and no one in my family likes turkey, so my parents, Andrew, and me keep it low key with a big chicken, some stuffing, and a few sides.

For our family, it's the day after Thanksgiving that feels more like a holiday. Black Friday is always the biggest day of the year for the gallery, so Dad offers free wine, hot chocolate, and cookies in the lobby; Mom holds an open house in the studio to give people a chance to dabble and apply for her art classes; and Andrew helps out behind the counter in the gift shop.

My job, though, is best of all. I set up a craft table next to the Christmas tree in the lobby and help kids cut out snowflakes to hang on the tree while their parents check out the art exhibits and shop. I may not be an artist, but snowflakes are my jam.

They come out perfectly symmetrical every time. And it's so fun to watch the kids' expressions as they unfold their flakes.

"Grab those scissors." I point to one of a half-dozen pairs of blunt-end scissors sitting on the table, and a boy named Bronwyn who appears to be about seven years old picks them up. I hand him his folded sheet of paper. "Here you go. You can do triangles or squares or circles or even little wavy lines. Whatever you want."

Bronwyn creases his forehead in concentration as he targets the upper left corner.

"Not too big. You don't want it to fall apart."

He snips a bit here and a bit there and then holds it out to me. "Is that good?"

"I think so. You ready to open it up?"

He nods, and together we unfold his sheet to discover a pinwheel-style flake.

His eyes dance. "Cool."

"Good job. Do you want to add sparkles?"

He shakes his head and wrinkles his nose.

"Okay, no sparkles. Do you want to keep it, or should we hang it on our tree?"

"Hang it!"

"Great." I circle the tree. "Let's find a good place for it."

"There's one." A voice behind me pipes up, and I turn to find Maggs pointing at a bare spot near the top of the tree.

"Maggs! You came!"

"You promised hot chocolate. Of course I came."

I run over and give her a hug. I had texted her and Brie, asking them to stop by. Maggs had said she'd try, but with Maggs, you can never be sure.

"Any word from … ?"

I shake my head. "Nothing. She hasn't said a word to me since dance class last week."

"She'll come around. If nothing else, her curiosity about what's going on with you and Darius will get the best of her." She tilts her head and gives me a side-eye. "Speaking of. What *is* going on with you and Darius?"

I nod toward my father, who is standing and watching us not five yards away. "Later. Right now, I need you to help this young man hang his snowflake while I run to the bathroom. And then both of you should definitely get some hot chocolate. Bronwyn, this is Maggs. Maggs, Bronwyn." I hand her the flake and take off down the hallway.

As soon as I get to the restroom, I pull out my phone and text Aiden.

Alicea: She's here. U coming?
Aiden: Yep. On my way.

I smile. This has to work. The two of them can bond over their love of art. We even have some new daisy prints in the gift shop.

I start to put away my phone, but another text pops up. It's from Darius.

Darius: OK if I bring Jaycee by to make some flakes?

My heart does a small flip. I so want to see him again. And kiss him. Especially kiss him. On the other hand, our relationship—or whatever it is—isn't exactly public yet. I'm not sure I want people to see us together. Besides, my mom and dad are both here, and they're going to be totally up in my business, and Andrew ... ugh, don't even get me started. The whole thing could get super awkward.

I squeeze my eyes shut and shake my head. *Less thinking, Alicea. More Darius.* My hands shaking, I text him back, telling him to stop by. With a smiley-face emoji for good measure.

I return to the lobby to find Maggs and Bronwyn drinking hot chocolate and talking to my dad, and a whole new crop of kids waiting at my table to make snowflakes. As I help them pick out their paper colors, I keep an eye on the front door.

When Aiden walks in, Maggs glances up from her hot chocolate, and her eyes widen a bit. "Hey. What are you doing here?" she asks.

He shrugs. "Christmas shopping for my mom."

"Aw. That's sweet."

I smile and hand a pair of scissors to one of the older kids. "I need you to supervise for a minute. I'll be right back."

I rush over and offer Aiden a drink. "We have some great new pieces hanging in the main gallery and a bunch of prints for sale in the store," I tell him. I nod to Maggs. "Why don't you go with him? Maybe you'll find something you like."

Maggs shoots me a confused look, but she follows Aiden down the hallway toward the shop.

I take a deep breath as I head back to the snowflake station. With a little luck, maybe Maggs will fall madly in love with Aiden. Or at the very least, maybe the two of them will hang out back there long enough for me to avoid awkward questions about Darius that even *I* don't know the answer to yet.

Chapter
THIRTY-THREE

Glitter, glitter everywhere. Gold, silver, pink, and blue. I've been here for less than two hours, and already I have it in my hair and all over my clothes. I'm helping a little girl clean it out from behind one of her ears when I hear his voice.

"Well, well. Isn't that the most beautiful angel you've ever seen?"

I look up to find Darius and Jaycee approaching my table. He's pointing to the angel on top of the tree, but his eyes are trained on me. My cheeks grow warm. "Hello."

"Hey."

"We're having a bit of a glitter emergency."

"So I see."

Jaycee grabs a wipe and practically pushes me out of the way as she crouches down and takes over on ear-cleaning duty.

"She's great with kids," Darius says. "She can't wait to

start babysitting."

I smile at him. "I'm glad you came." I am. It's only been two days, but I realize I've missed him. His smile, his voice, his eyes, his hair. I desperately want to reach up and touch those curls. My mind flashes to the art supply closet by my mom's studio. So tempting, but I shake away the thought. "Want to make a snowflake?"

Darius grins. "Of course. That's what we're here for." He grabs the pile of papers and begins sorting through to pick out a color.

I'm curious to see what kind of flake he'll make.

"Want to know my favorite thing about snowflakes?" I ask.

"What's that?"

"They're perfect every time."

He laughs. "Right. Of course." His expression turns mischievous. "Unless ... " He pulls out an ice-blue sheet, holds it up, and slowly and very deliberately creates an uneven fold. "You do this."

"What! You wouldn't."

"Oh, I would." He lowers his voice. "I am."

I reach out to grab the sheet from him, but he pulls it away.

"What kind of monster are you?"

"I'm your worst nightmare."

I purse my lips and glare. "Fine. Go ahead and make your imperfect flake. But don't expect me to hang it on the tree with all the perfect ones."

"We'll see about that." He picks up a pair of scissors and chops away, cutting bits and pieces off the sides, the corners, and the offending sticking-out part. He pays no attention to what he's doing. Instead, he stares at me, his grin mocking me with each snip, snip, snip. Finally, with a great flourish, he opens it up.

It is perhaps the most hideous snowflake I've ever seen. "Um. Wow."

Jaycee stands up and smirks at her brother. "What the—? That is *not* how it's done."

Darius hugs the monstrosity to his chest. "You people have no appreciation for art."

"It's weird and crooked," she says.

"And? What's wrong with weird and crooked?" He holds the flake out to me. "Go ahead. Hang it. I dare you."

"You dare me? Really? Isn't that just a pitiful attempt to get me to hang something you know doesn't deserve to be hung?"

Darius laughs. "Maybe." He holds the snowflake up to my face. "I double dare you."

"Oh, okay. Now you've got me." I snatch it from him and eye the tree. "I know exactly where this belongs." I walk around to the far side, by the wall, where the plug for the lights is buried.

"Oh no you don't. You're not hiding my masterpiece back there." Darius chases after me. He grabs for the flake, but I hold it away. He reaches around me, his arm circling my waist.

I know Jaycee is a few feet from us and my father is across the room, but I can't help myself. We're hidden by the tree, and so I kiss him—a quick, teasing peck. Only the brief sensation of his lips on mine makes me want more, so

I lean into him. "What are you willing to do for this flake?" I murmur.

His eyebrows shoot up, and his gaze sweeps over me. "Do you really want to know?"

"I do."

"You're sure?"

"I am."

"And you want me to do it, right here, right now?"

My heart skips a beat. "I dare you."

He shrugs. "Okay. You asked for it." At which point he tilts his head back and belts out an ear-splitting falsetto version of "Let It Go." By the time he pauses and whispers the line about how, "The cold never bothered me anyway," I am a puddle of giggles.

"You win," I say when I finally catch my breath. "Here." I hand him the flake. "Hang it wherever you want."

He grins, takes it from me, and leads me back around to the front of the tree ... where apparently his singing has attracted a curious audience. About a dozen people are gathered in the lobby staring at us. Including Maggs and Aiden. And Brie.

"Um. Hello, everyone."

Super awkward. Yep. Called it.

Chapter
THIRTY-FOUR

I rush over to my friends, head up and shoulders back, trying my best to look as though I didn't just kiss Darius Groves behind the Christmas tree in the lobby of my parents' art gallery.

"Thanks for coming, Brie. I'm really glad you're here."

"Sure." Brie regards me with a wary expression and a pasted-on smile. "I wasn't expecting a concert," she says, turning toward Darius. "Has anyone ever told you that you have an amazing voice?"

He shakes his head.

"Yeah, well. There's a reason for that."

Darius laughs, as do the rest of us, and for one brief moment, the awkwardness disappears.

Until Brie turns to Maggs and Aiden. "So, you two are … ?"

Maggs blinks. "Um. No. I mean, we're not … anything.

I'm just … I'm here for the hot chocolate."

"Same here." Aiden gives a jittery laugh. "I mean, not the part about the hot chocolate. I'm here for a present for my mom."

I eye Maggs. She seems nervous, in a protesteth-too-much kind of way. Maybe this thing with Aiden is working. Meanwhile, Aiden keeps glancing back and forth between Darius and me, as though he's trying to piece things together.

Darius has remained standing over by the tree, snowflake in hand, clearly unsure whether he should join us. I want to call him over, but I don't. Somehow it feels as though doing so would make the whole thing real. It would be like flipping a switch. I'm not sure I'm ready for Darius to go from being a kiss-in-a-closet to being my boyfriend. Or at least, I'm not sure I'm ready to reveal that to Aiden—and by extension the entire Grand View High School student body.

Instead, I turn to Brie and pull her toward the back of the lobby. "We need to talk. I'm really sorr—"

"It's okay." Brie stops me. "You don't need to apologize. It's just that you and Maggs are … I don't know. Sometimes I feel like I'm on the outside. I know it's probably because I spend so much time with Blake, and sometimes I open my mouth when I shouldn't, so I get it. It's cool. We're cool."

"No." I grab both her arms. "That's not cool. I don't want you feeling like you're on the outside."

"But I am."

"No, you're not."

"I am."

"Brie, no, you're—"

"Then why would you keep a secret from me?"

I open my mouth, but I have no reply. She's got me there.

"Secrets are for people who are on the inside. Where I am not."

I let her go, and my shoulders sag. She has a point.

Then I remember. "You and I have a secret."

"What secret?"

"You know. About … " I nod toward Maggs and Aiden.

"That's not the same. That's matchmaking stuff."

"I know, but … " I sigh. "Brie, I swear, I was going to tell you about the whole Darius thing. I just … I needed to work it out more myself."

"And so? Have you?"

"Have I what?"

"Worked it out?"

I glance over at Darius, who has turned his attention to Jaycee and is helping her pick out glitter for her star. "Yes. No." I shake my head. "I don't know."

Brie gives a huge sigh. "Honestly, Alicea. You need to make up your—"

"Okay. See? This is what I'm talking about." I wave my hand in front of her face. "This is what you do."

Brie stands with her mouth open. I can tell she's dying to spit out her thoughts on my dating ineptitude, but to her credit, she checks herself. "You're right. I'm sorry. Not my place."

"Thank you."

"But I do want to say … "

I shoot her a warning glare.

She leans toward me and whispers, "He really likes you. I can tell. And that's worth something."

Chapter
THIRTY-FIVE

Mood: Determined.

I walk into calc class Monday morning with a purpose. Brie's right. The fact that Darius likes me is worth something. And there's no denying I like him back. He's super sweet and protective of his sister, funny, has a lot of surprising talents, and—well, yeah—there are the curls and the kissing.

I thought about it all weekend and have made my decision. Today, in calc, I'm flipping the switch. And I don't care if the whole Grand View High student body knows it.

I approach Darius's desk. "Hey."

He looks up, his eyes widening with surprise.

The girl at the desk next to his stares at me, a smirk spreading across her face. Someone a few rows away snickers. I hesitate. My mind flashes to my past with Ty, when most of the girls I passed in the hallway eyed me with envy.

"What's up?" Darius's voice brings me back to my present, and one look into his eyes reminds me of exactly what I'm doing.

"I wanted to see whether you'd like to get some coffee after school today." I say this loud enough to make sure everyone can hear me. *Switch. Flipped.*

He grins. "Sure."

"Okay, then. See you at Cuppa's." I feel twenty-three sets of eyes following me as I walk back up the aisle toward my desk. With each step, doubt creeps back in. I know what they're all thinking. It's the same thing I thought when I first saw Darius's name on Brie's cell screen. A major step down. The Anti-Ty.

Ignore them, Alicea. This isn't about them.

As I take my seat, my phone buzzes in my back pocket.

Darius: Your chai's on me.

I smile. This isn't about them at all.

"Congratulations!" Maggs hops up from her seat at the lunch table and gives Brie a hug.

"Well, it's not MIT," Brie says, glancing my way. "But it is my second choice, after Virginia, of course, which I probably won't get into and which my parents can't exactly afford. Still, I'll be an hour closer to UVA, so … James Madison, here I come." She pumps her fist in the air. "Go Duke Dogs."

Maggs clasps her hands together, her eyes misty. "I can't believe this time next year we'll all be separated."

I shrug. "That's what FaceTime is for."

"I know, but it won't be the same. Who's going to give me a hard time every morning about putting butter in my coffee?"

"At St. John's?" Brie asks. "Probably no one. In fact, all your counter-culture comrades may be drinking it right along with you. Or even weirder stuff."

"It's not weird. It boosts energy," Maggs says.

"Right." We've heard this many times before. Something about the wonders of Tibetan yak butter tea, never mind the fact that (a) we're in America, (b) she's using cow butter, and (c) it's coffee.

"It does," she insists. "And besides, just because I'm going to a liberal arts college doesn't mean everyone there will be weird."

"It kind of does," Brie says. "They'll all be philosophy and lit weird, as opposed to wherever Alicea is going, where they'll all be computer-geek weird." She holds up her hands as we glare. "Both of which are awesome kinds of weird. You know I love you."

"What makes you think you're the arbiter of normal?" I say.

"I'm not. I'm weird, too, in fact. I'm … weird-friends weird." She laughs and ducks as Maggs throws a granola bar and I toss a carrot stick at her. "Kidding. Kidding."

I toss another one at her for good measure. To be honest, I'm so relieved things are back to normal with us, she could call me weird all day long and I wouldn't mind.

"Speaking of computer-geek weird." Maggs turns to me. "Did you get your MIT application in?"

I nod and hold up crossed fingers. "Finished it this weekend. I hope my essay was good enough."

"I'm sure it was great. Because Libby is great."

"What was that?" I cup my hand to my ear. "Could you say that again? Did you just call Libby great?"

Maggs laughs. "Don't get too excited. I still don't think a computer can calculate true love. But yes, she's great. She's brilliant. Because you're brilliant."

Yeah, well. Based on how you were acting around Aiden the other day, maybe she's better than you think. I'm dying to say it, but I don't. If Maggs knew Aiden was her match, she might sabotage whatever they've got going simply to prove a point. Instead, I take a deep breath. Time to tell Maggs and Brie about what happened in calc.

"So guess what I did this… whoa." I stop and nod toward Ty's lunch table. "Do you see what I see?"

Maggs and Brie follow my gaze.

"What?"

"I don't see anything."

"You mean Ty? What about him?" Maggs squints. "Did he get his hair cut?"

"No. He's *sans* Becca. And today is a B Day." I stand and scan the room, finally spotting her at a table full of football players, giggling at something one of them is saying and draping herself around his arm. "Well, well. She appears to have switched teams. Literally. This is an interesting turn of events."

Brie rolls her eyes at me. "Honestly, Alicea, you need to get over that boy. Move on. He's not worth it."

I bristle at Brie's tone but say nothing. We've finally patched things up between us, and besides, she kind of has a point. "I merely said it was interesting. And for your information, I am moving on. This morning in calc, I asked Darius out. Kind of."

"What?" They squeal in unison, and I tell them what happened.

"Oh my gosh." Maggs squirms in her seat with excitement. "Why are we just now learning about this? Why didn't you tell us the second we got here?"

"I didn't want to step on Brie's news. Which, let's face it, is bigger than my news."

"Barely." Brie grins at me. "Now, if I got into Virginia, that would be huge news. And who knows? If Alicea Springer can get past her infatuation with Ty Walker, I feel like *anything* is possible."

The two of them spend the next eight minutes arguing over whether coffee at Cuppa Joe counts as a first date (Maggs says definitely, Brie says not quite), before the bell finally rings.

Maggs gives me a hug as we head out. "Have fun. I can't wait to hear how it goes."

"Thanks. I'll tell you all about it." First date or not, I'm looking forward to going out with Darius, and I'm happy that Maggs and Brie are so excited for me.

Still, I can't help but glance back at Ty, all alone as he walks down the hall toward his next class.

Chapter
THIRTY-SIX

When I was little, a friend let me play with her paint-by-numbers set. I painted a giant monarch butterfly atop a bright pink-and-purple bloom. I loved seeing the picture come to life beneath my brush, the colors so brilliant and their placement within the lines so precise.

I brought the picture home and hid it in a drawer. I knew my parents and brother would laugh. Calling something a "paint-by-number" was the epitome of an insult for the Springers. But every once in a while, in the privacy of my room, I would take out the painting and admire my handiwork. I knew even then that art was not my thing, but I felt a certain pride in that piece. It was pretty, happy, and vivid. I named the butterfly Elizabeth, after the queen of England.

The painting hanging above our booth at Cuppa Joe

reminds me a bit of that picture. It's been years since I've dug it out, but I remember its every detail. "What do you think of that butterfly?" I ask Darius.

He glances at it and looks back at me, confused. "What do you mean?"

"It's pretty, isn't it?"

He shrugs. "Sure. Most butterflies are."

"Exactly. They're beautiful."

A look of realization crosses his face and he laughs. "I see. It's because they're symmetrical, isn't it?"

"No. Well, maybe. I didn't think of that, but now that you mention it, it doesn't hurt." I lean across the table toward him. "I just mean that a painting can be simple—it can be something as common and maybe even as cliché as a butterfly—and still be something pretty to hang on your wall. It doesn't always have to be … *Art*."

Darius tilts his head. "You say 'art' like it's a bad thing."

"Not a bad thing. More like … an unknowable thing. I mean, what makes one painting 'art' and another 'not art'? And who's to judge?"

He takes a sip of his coffee, and I can see him turning the question over in his mind. Finally, he sets down his cup. "You know what they say: Beauty is in the eye of the beholder. I think that goes for art, as well. So you can call cliché butterfly paintings art if you want."

I smile. "Good. I do. I declare Queen Elizabeth up there a work of art."

"Queen Eliz—? Ah, because she's a monarch."

I tap his cup with mine. "Exactly. And speaking of works of art … " I stare at him expectantly.

"It's almost ready. I swear. One more class—maybe two—and I'll be finished. Then you can see it. At this point, though, I'm kind of worried it won't live up to the hype. I think I need to lower your expectations."

"Oh, it's too late for that. My expectations are very high, I assure you."

He shakes his head. "Then you may be in for a disappointment."

"And whose fault would that be? You could have shown it to me weeks ago, but no, you insisted I had to wait until it was perfect."

"Not perfect. Ready."

"What's the difference?"

"There is a difference. I told you, perfection is not my goal. If I worried about making everything perfect, I'd never create anything. Or at least, I'd never finish anything."

I purse my lips and quirk an eyebrow at him.

"And I *am* going to finish it."

"So you say."

"I swear. It's really close." He laughs and grabs my hand as I set down my cup and squeezes my pinkie finger. "And then I will show it to you. A promise is a promise."

His touch sends a shiver up my arm, and I realize my tea doesn't interest me nearly as much as his curls. I am itching to tangle my fingers in them.

He narrows his eyes as though he's reading my mind and nods toward the door. "I have an idea. Are you ready to go?"

My stomach feels as though Queen Elizabeth and a dozen of her friends have taken flight inside.

"Ready."

Chapter
THIRTY-SEVEN

"Sorry, Brie, but Maggs wins. That totally counted as a first date." I lift my foot onto the barre and stretch out over my leg, extending my arm over my ear.

Brie peers up at me from her deep *plié* and grins. "Oh? Do go on."

I shake my head. "Sorry. Nice girls don't kiss and tell."

Maggs and Brie both inch closer to me.

"So there was kissing. And … ?"

"Nothing. Just kissing." But I smile, because it was some *awesome* kissing.

After we left Cuppa Joe, Darius and I drove to Claymore Park, where he challenged me to a competition on the monkey bars. I think I surprised him. He had strength, but I had agility. After my final spin around the bars, ending with a soaring dismount, I gave him a high-five that somehow morphed into an embrace.

"Impressive," he whispered, his lips inches from mine. "You fly like an angel. I take it your neck is feeling better?"

"Much." I reached up and touched it. "Hasn't hurt in days." His hairline was damp, adding tiny curls to his bigger curls, and I swiped at them. "You worked up a sweat doing those pull-ups."

"That's because I did ... how many?"

"Sixteen." I'd bet he couldn't do more than a dozen. "Not sure that last one counted, though."

"Fine. Fifteen and a half. I still win the bet."

"Yes, you do," I admitted. "What do I owe you?"

He tilted his head, as though considering his options. "Sixteen kisses?"

"Hmm. I don't know. Maybe fifteen and a half."

"That works." And with that, he pulled me close and kissed me for what might have been fifteen and a half kisses, although I can't be sure. It simultaneously felt like an infinite number and yet left me wanting more. Too soon, he pulled away.

"We should go," he said, his voice rough. "It's getting dark."

"I don't mind the dark."

"Okay, but I think we should—"

"I'll bet you can't do ten pushups."

"Oh, no you don't. I'm not falling for that."

"Please." I gave him my best, most irresistible pout, and he slowly, softly touched his lips to mine, for one last glorious kiss that sent a thrill all the way through me and made me feel as though I was indeed flying like an—

"Circle up, ladies." Ms. DuBois's clap-clap-clap brings me tumbling back into class. Today, for the first time, we're going to dance the "Waltz of the Flowers." We've spent the past three sessions walking through it, learning the choreography and figuring out how to match our movements to the music. I've been practicing my solo pieces on my own, but this will be the first time I've performed them in front of all the other girls, and the monarchs have once again invaded my belly.

Ms. DuBois pokes my breastbone. "Butterflies are good. Use them." The woman's a mind reader.

I close my eyes and take a deep breath, allowing the soft sounds of the violin in the first measure of the waltz to relax me, and then it's game on. I'm in a zone, and I nail every move. My *plié* is deeper than ever, my *jeté* higher, my *brisé* sharper, and my *foetté* turns draw more than a few admiring glances from my classmates. Partway through the dance, though, Ms. DuBois steps onto the floor.

"Alicea, *s'il vous plaît.*"

I stop, surprised. "What's wrong?"

"Nothing." She walks around me, slowly, eyeing me from head to toe. "Nothing is wrong. Your steps and your positioning are perfect and precise. But I am not seeing Dewdrop."

"Excuse me?"

"A minute ago, when I walked into the room, I saw Dewdrop. In your face, in your eyes. Now she is gone."

Behind us, Brie snickers.

Ms. DuBois turns to her. "What is the joke, Brietta?"

Brie shakes her head, but then starts laughing. "That wasn't Dewdrop, Ms. DuBois. That was the look of looooove."

This sends a wave of giggles through the class, and even Ms. DuBois cracks a smile.

"Well, then. Love works, too." She points at me as she exits the floor. "Perhaps you should work on that."

158

Chapter
THIRTY-EIGHT

B rie has overstated the situation. I am *not* in love with Darius Groves, never mind the fact that I'm drawing a million hearts around his name in my lit notebook at the moment.

Mr. Dunham hovers over my desk. "Alicea, why do you think Teasdale uses sea grass as an analogy in this poem?"

I cover my doodles with my hand and look up. Our class is analyzing "I Would Live in Your Love" by Sara Teasdale. The verse is on the white board:

I would live in your love as the sea-grasses live in the sea,
Borne up by each wave as it passes, drawn down by each wave that recedes;
I would empty my soul of the dreams that have gathered in me,
I would beat with your heart as it beats, I would follow your soul as it leads.

I glance around at my classmates. Poetry has never been my strong suit—too much ambiguity. Still, this verse seems obvious. "Because sea grass needs the sea," I say. "It can't live anywhere else. It's like she can't live without him. Just like the title says … I would live in your love."

Mr. Dunham turns and strolls back to his desk. He perches on the edge of it, removes his glasses, and points them at me. "And what do you think about that?" he asks. "About living in someone's love?"

I shrug. I think it's romantic—being swept up by the waves and becoming someone's soul mate. It's what finding your perfect match is supposed to be all about. Still, I don't say this, because I'm hyper-aware of Darius and Ty and everyone else watching me. "It's cool," I reply. "I like it."

"Fair enough." Mr. Dunham peers around the room. "Other thoughts? Does anyone have a different interpretation of the poem?"

Abi Eisenberg raises her hand. "I don't think it's cool at all," she says. "I think it's creepy."

Mr. Dunham nods. "Okay. Explain."

"She's not writing about love. She's writing about obsession." Abi trains her eyes on me. "Real love doesn't mean drowning yourself in the other person. 'I would empty my soul of the dreams that have gathered in me.' What's that about?"

Mr. Dunham turns toward me. "What do you have to say to that?"

I'm not sure whether he's expecting me to defend Teasdale or myself. When I speak, my voice is small and strangled. "Abi has a point."

"So what do the rest of you think?" he asks the class. "Is this love or obsession?"

"That depends." Darius answers from the back. I turn, surprised. It's not like him to speak up.

Mr. Dunham walks down the row toward him. "Depends on what?"

"Not on what; on who," Darius says. "With the right person, it's not about drowning, it's about thriving—growing thick and strong like sea grass. Maybe she says she'd empty her soul of her dreams because they were the wrong dreams."

I steal a glance at Abi, who is staring at Darius with her mouth agape. The look in her eyes is pure respect. She catches my eye and offers a slight but meaningful head tilt.

Mr. Dunham heads back up the aisle, his eyes once again on me, but mercifully, the bell rings before he can call on me again. As I jump up and head out the door, Darius appears at my side.

"Hey, Bright Angel."

I fall into step beside him. "Not sure why Dunham decided to pick on me today. That was annoying."

"He tends to call on people who aren't paying attention."

I elbow him in the side. "What's that supposed to mean?"

"I don't know. You seemed engrossed in your notebook. What were you writing?"

I blush at the thought of my heart drawings. "Nothing. Just doodling."

Darius glances at my armload of books, and for a moment I fear he's going to try to snatch it from me, but he merely grins. "If you say so."

We walk in silence, stopping at my locker.

"So I was thinking … " Darius leans toward me, his voice low. "Maybe we could take another field trip to Claymore Park after school. I bet I can make the full sixteen pull-ups this time."

I smile. "What are the stakes?"

"The same as the other day."

"Ah. So if you win, I have to kiss you. And if I win?"

He shrugs. "That's up to you. But it doesn't matter, because you won't." He walks backward away from me down the hallway. "Because I'm motivated to collect my prize. Very, very motivated."

I watch him until he rounds the corner, and I have to remind myself to breathe as I turn to open my locker and dig through it for my physics book.

"So how long have you two been a thing?"

I look up to find Michelle Randall and Lauren Cooke staring at me. Neither of them has spoken more than a few words to me in our three and a half years at Grand View, and I'm pretty sure this is the first time they've acknowledged my existence since my break-up with Ty.

I shrug. "It's pretty new."

"Isn't that … sweet?" Lauren's tone oozes fake.

"I wouldn't have pegged you as a Darius Groves kind of girl," Michelle says.

"Excuse me?"

"I just mean … " She leans in and lowers her voice. "I feel like you could do better."

And with that, the two of them take off into the crowd, Lauren's faux giggle rising above the din.

Seriously? Did that just happen? Part of me wishes I had

stood up to them—stood up for Darius—and explained how much he makes me laugh, and how sweet he can be, and how he may not be perfect but he's a better person than they ever will be. But another part of me knows that not too long ago, I felt the same way they do. And a teeny, tiny part of me still fears that maybe they're right.

Chapter
THIRTY-NINE

The next couple of weeks fly by in a whirlwind of schoolwork, dance classes, and more than a few visits to Claymore Park. I'm so busy, I barely have time to notice the occasional stares and snickers that trail after me through Grand View's hallways. Still, I do notice, and while I wish I could say it didn't bother me, a girl can only handle so much snark.

Maybe that's why I'm a bit jumpy one Friday morning when I feel a tap on my shoulder while I'm standing at my locker.

"What do you ... want?" My voice goes from a shout to a strangled whisper as I turn to find Ty standing behind me, a giant candy cane in his hand.

"Hey. Can we talk?"

I open my mouth, but nothing comes out, so I nod instead.

"I've been thinking about you a lot lately, and I wondered

if … Alicea, are you okay?"

I can't take my eyes off the candy cane. I'm having a major flashback, with all the feelings I had a year ago—shock, excitement, and the general giddiness that goes with having a years-long fantasy come to life—except now they're mixed with something else. Disorientation. Confusion.

"I'm fine," I say finally. "Is that for me?"

"Oh, yeah. It is." He hands me the candy cane, and I grasp it so tightly it cracks.

"Where are you heading?"

"Calculus."

"Can I walk you?"

"Um. No." My brain is whirling, and I have to lean back against my locker to stay upright. Is this for real? I'm not sure what to think or feel, and I have no idea what's about to happen, but I do know one thing: I don't want Darius around to see it. "Actually, let's just talk here. If that's okay."

"Sure." He leans against the locker beside mine. "So I wanted to ask you … I have tickets to see the Factory Boys at the 9:30 Club tonight, and I know it's kind of short notice, but I thought maybe it would be fun, and—"

"I don't think so, Ty." My throat is so tight, I can barely say the words. "I mean, that's really nice, but the timing … "

"I know. Like I said. Short notice."

I nod, though that wasn't what I meant.

"The thing is … " He leans in and lowers his voice. "My dad got these tickets from work. They're in the third row, and there are a bunch of them, so you could invite some friends—including Maggs and Aiden. I know you've been trying to get those two together."

I stare at his piercing eyes, the ones I've allowed myself to get lost in for almost four years, and that brilliant smile that still sends a thrill up my spine. "I don't know."

"Come on. It'll be fun." He puts his hand around mine and the now-crumbling candy cane. "I know you love the Factory Boys."

I do, it's true. And I have been running out of ways to get Maggs and Aiden in the same room. And then there's the way he's holding my …

I pull my hand away and take a step back. "Let me think about it."

He grins. "Sure. Enjoy the candy cane."

I avoid Darius's gaze all through calculus. When the bell rings, he walks up to my desk, but I tell him I need to run to the bathroom. I take the long way to the rest of my morning classes so I won't run into him.

Finally, lunchtime arrives. Maggs and Brie are already at our table when I walk in.

"Where have you been?" Maggs asks.

"G Hall," I mutter.

"Why would you be all the way over in—"

"Ty gave me a candy cane." I blurt it out, panic in my voice.

Brie reacts as I knew she would, lips puckered, eyebrows raised. "Please tell me you're kidding."

"Brie." Maggs shoots her a warning look, but it does no good.

"I can't even. Alicea, you've been happier for the past few weeks than the entire time I've known you. And that includes last year when you were dating Mr. Golden Boy. Please tell me you handed the candy cane back to him and told him where he could shove it."

"No. I did not." I take it out of my backpack and hold it out for her to see.

"It's in pieces."

"It was whole when he gave it to me."

She sighs, a long, dramatic sigh. "Okay. So what does this mean?"

"I don't know. I'm not sure what to think. I had pretty much given up on ever getting back together with him, but then he goes and does this, and … you have to admit, it's kind of sweet that he remembered about the candy cane."

"Yeah. Though if I recall, the last time didn't end so well."

I glare at her. Brie knows how heartbroken our breakup left me. She knows as well as anyone that I don't need to be reminded of it. "Seriously? Thanks for the support."

"Alicea." Maggs drapes her arm around my shoulder and squeezes. "You know Brie's just—"

"Yes. I do know. I also know she has a point. That doesn't make it any less hurtful."

"Sorry," Brie mutters.

We sit for a moment in silence, until Maggs clears her throat. "Well, I think the candy cane *is* kind of sweet. What did he say when he gave it to you?"

"Oh, I almost forgot." I sit up a little straighter. "He asked me to go see the Factory Boys tonight. He has a bunch of tickets, so both of you could go, and Blake, too, since he's in town. He's also inviting some other friends. I think Aiden might be there." I glance at Brie as if to say, *See? This isn't all about me. There may be an opportunity to do some good here.*

"Well, that's nice of him," Maggs says. "So it would be more of a group thing."

"Right. An outing. Not necessarily a date, per se."

"And what about Darius?" Brie asks.

I close my eyes. It's a question I've pushed out of my mind all morning. What about him? What about us? Because I can call this a "group thing" or an "outing" or whatever I want, but we all know it's still suspiciously date-like. "Darius is awesome, and sweet, and funny, and I really like him, but he's … not Ty." I let out a long moan. "What should I do?"

Brie snorts. "You know what I think."

I turn to Maggs, whose eyes widen. "Don't ask me. I'm the queen of indecision." She takes my hand in hers. "But whatever you decide, I'll support you. We both will."

She nudges Brie, who again snorts. "Alicea plus Ty equals A-Lie."

I stick my tongue out. "And Brie plus Blake equals Break, but you two seem to be doing just fine."

"Yeah, well, Blake's not an idi—"

"Come on, you two," Maggs pleads with us. "Don't fight. I think we all want the same thing here, which is for Alicea to be happy."

Brie rolls her eyes. "Fine. And if Alicea insists Ty will make her happy, I'll try to be supportive. Or at least, I won't puke all over her like I want to right now."

I can't help but smile. "Deal." That's the best I'll get from her anyway.

Chapter FORTY

LIBBY Question #61: Your guilty pleasure involves:

A. Sweets
B. Reality TV
C. Boy bands
D. Show tunes

Both Ty and I picked "C." No surprise there. Back when we were dating, I once caught Ty jamming to a One Direction song in his car, bobbing and weaving and shimmying as though he were Harry himself. It was seriously one of the most adorable things I'd ever witnessed.

I smile at the memory as I hop into the shower. I've accepted Ty's offer to see the Factory Boys and have spent the past five hours shuttling back and forth on a bridge between

Thrillsville and Guiltberg. With the exception of a couple of texts, I've managed to avoid Darius. He hinted at getting together this weekend, but I told him I have a lot stuff to do to get ready for Christmas.

I close my eyes and let the heat from the shower seep into my body. It's just a concert, a night out with friends. Besides, don't I owe it to myself to see whether Ty and I could still have a connection? I've invested way too much time and energy in him to simply walk away.

My phone rings, so I shut off the water, grab my towel, and answer. It's Maggs.

"What are you wearing tonight?"

"What?"

Maggs never seems to care much about her own clothes, much less what other people are wearing.

"I'm trying to decide between my pink-and-yellow paisley dress and a black ribbed sweater. What do people wear to Factory Workers concerts, anyway?"

"Factory Boys." Boy bands are *not* Maggs's guilty pleasure. I wrap the towel around my body and another one around my head and skitter across the hall to my room. "Say it with me. Fac-tor-y Boys. Have you been listening to their Pandora channel?"

"For the past two hours. Which honestly, has felt like two years. I mean, really? 'We're a sure thing. Like fellas in the cold.' What does that even mean?"

"It's Phelps. As in Michael."

"What?"

"'We're a sure thing. Like Phelps winning gold.'"

"Oh." She giggles. "That makes a lot more sense. But still.

It's all so … be-boppity. Remind me again why I'm going to see them."

"Because you're a great friend." *And—even though you won't admit it—because you want to hang out with Aiden.*

"Alicea?" Maggs's voice is soft.

"Yeah?"

"I know Brie and I haven't always been super fans where Ty's concerned, but that's just because … you know."

"The epic dumping?"

"Yeah, that. And also, I felt like … "

"What is it? Tell me."

She sighs. "I mean, you've been trying to get back together with him for so long, and he kept going out with those other girls. I guess I wanted you to move on, too."

"Wow. Have I really seemed that desperate?"

"Come on. Don't take it like that. You know that's not what I mean. And anyway, obviously I was wrong. Because he asked you to this concert, so clearly he does still like you. And if you really, truly want to get back together with him, I'm behind you all the way."

"Thank you."

"So do you?"

I lie down on my bed and pull the towel off of my hair and over my face. "I don't know. Which is crazy. A month ago, this would have been a dream come true. But now … "

"Because of Darius."

It's a statement, not a question, so I don't respond. I close my eyes and take a deep breath and tell myself that everything will turn out fine and we'll have a good time tonight. I'll figure all this stuff out later.

"I gotta get ready, Maggs. See you in an hour. Oh, and go with the paisley. 'Cause that's what you wear to a … what concert is it?"

"Factory Boys."

"Good job, Maggs."

Chapter
FORTY-ONE

Ty looks super cute in his Messi jersey when he and Aiden pick me up.

Aiden hops out and holds the passenger-side door for me. "You can ride shotgun."

"Oh, you are *such* a gentleman," I say. "You sure you'll be okay in the back with Maggs?"

His laughs, his face reddening.

I point at him. "No blushing once we pick her up. Do you understand? I think she's starting to really like you, but you need to play it cool. If she suspects this is a set-up, she'll shut it down."

Ty flashes a wide smile as I sit down next to him. I went with a short, flouncy red dress, black tights, and tan ankle boots. "Hi. Thanks again for the tickets. And for offering to drive."

"Of course. You look really pretty."

The way he's gazing at me makes me feel simultaneously charmed and traitorous, so I bite my lip and turn my attention to my phone. "Let me text Brie to let her know we're on our way. She and Blake said they'd meet us there."

When we get to Maggs's house, she emerges wearing the paisley dress. She raises her eyebrows when she sees the seating arrangements but climbs into the back next to Aiden without comment.

"So are you a big Factory Boys fan, Maggs?" Ty asks as we pull out of her neighborhood and head toward D.C.

"Oh, yeah. The biggest." Her tone drips with sarcasm. "Dakota is my favorite."

"Dakota?"

"You know. The one with the side shave."

"You mean Montana."

Maggs laughs. "Dakota, Montana, whatever. I knew it was one of those cowboy states."

"Pop isn't really Maggs's thing," I say. "Though I have a feeling she's going to be all in after tonight. She'll want to join the Assembly Line for sure."

"The Assembly Line?" Maggs asks. "Is that what they call their fans?"

"I don't think it was their idea." Ty says. "More like a Twitter thing."

"Hashtag Assembly Line!" I flash Maggs a smile. "Seriously, I think you're going to have a blast. Did I mention we're in the third row? We'll be able to count the grooves in Montana's side shave." I turn to Aiden. "And what do you think? Are you a fan?"

He shrugs. "They're okay. I'm more of a Phish kind of guy."

I nod and pretend not to notice how wide Maggs's eyes have gotten at the mention of her favorite band. "I think we're going to have to convert these two," I say as I turn Ty's stereo to a Factory Boys playlist.

Ty laughs and pumps up the volume, and together we sing the second verse of "Throwing Shade." *Beware that smile, that adoring gaze. Don't you know she's a double-edged blade? Her smile's so sweet but she's throwing shade.*

I gaze out at the skyscrapers as we drive by Tyson's Corner and try to relax back into my seat. This is just like old times. It's what I've dreamed of ever since the breakup. It's almost pure bliss. Almost.

The first three rows at the 9:30 Club are made up mostly of screaming girls, and Maggs, Brie, and I join the hysteria as the band takes the stage. They open with "Dream About You," which is a song even Maggs and Aiden know, because you'd have to be living in Antarctica not to. *I want to close my eyes. It's all I want to do. 'Cause when I dream, girl, I dream about you. Your eyes, your lips, your sweet curvy lines. And in my dreams, I make you mine, so fine.*

We all jump and sing and dance together, and I can't stop

smiling. Three girls in the row in front of us keep turning around to check out Ty. One of them gives me a once-over, pure admiration in her eyes.

In an instant, I'm transported back to last year. I'd been a nobody for so long, I practically blended in with the rows of tan metal lockers lining the halls of Grand View. But when Ty showed up with that first candy cane, I became a somebody. Now, dancing next to him, I feel that way again. These girls noticed me. They want to trade places with me. They want to *be* me.

At the end of the first set, the band slows things down with "Never Forget," and we chill into our seats. I'm flushed from all the dancing, and so is Ty. I lean sideways toward him so our shoulders touch, my focus on Wilson as he croons into his mic. "So, what do you think?" I ask. "Are you having fun?"

Ty leans in to me. "Definitely. Are you?"

I glance at him, and he smiles, and the whole world seems to stop for a second. His smile has always made me feel as though I'm the only girl in the room, and this is a big room. With lots of girls. "I miss you." It's out of my mouth before I realize I've said it. My face grows warm, and seconds feel like hours as I wait for his reaction.

He nods. "Me too."

I turn back toward the stage. *Him too.*

Wilson walks toward us and leans out over the crowd. I swear he looks straight into my eyes. "Like the sea and the sky and the mountains high. My love for you will never die. Never forget. Never forget. Baby, baby, never forget."

Chapter FORTY-TWO

After the concert, Ty drops off Aiden first and then Maggs. Since he and Aiden live practically in the same neighborhood, he clearly wants some time alone with me.

Is he going to tell me again that he misses me? Kiss me? Say he wants me back? As we drive through my neighborhood, past the festive red, green and white Christmas lights hanging from my neighbors' trees, my head swims with the possibilities.

Ty pulls up to my house and cuts the engine. I unbuckle my seatbelt and shift toward him, curling my left leg up under me on the seat.

"Thanks for coming tonight," he says.

"Thanks for bringing me. I had fun."

"Me too. That's why I wanted to drop you off last."

"Oh?" I say this as though I hadn't noticed.

He takes my hand in his and fiddles with my bracelet. He won't look at me. It's almost as though he's nervous. I don't believe I've ever seen Ty nervous. Finally he meets my gaze, his eyes guarded. "I meant it when I said I missed you. Lately I've been thinking. I don't know if it's too late, but … " He takes a deep breath. "I want to get back together."

I bite my bottom lip. I have imagined this conversation so many times, it's like reading a script. "You do?"

"I do."

"I did, too."

His forehead creases. "Did?"

I blink. *Did?* That's not in the script. "It's just … I mean—"

"It's because of him, isn't it? Darius."

The sound of his name elicits a pang of guilt. I've worked hard for the past few hours to put Darius out of my mind. To give Ty and me a chance. And I have to admit, tonight has been a blast. It's been fun and exciting and exhilarating, and I've felt exactly the way I did when I was Ty Walker's girlfriend. Until …

"Ty?"

He lets go of my bracelet and weaves his fingers through mine. "What is it?"

"Last year. Why did you … you know?"

He closes his eyes.

"I mean, I know you said there was nobody else, but I've always kind of thought maybe—"

"No." He shakes his head. "I know it probably seemed that way because I turned around and hooked up. But that wasn't planned. And it was a mistake." He looks me in the eye. "When I said there was no one else, I was being honest. I was just … an idiot, basically. I didn't know what I wanted."

I nod. "Okay."

"So what do you think? You and me? Can we start over?"

I lean the side of my head against my seat and take him in. He is every bit as gorgeous as the first day I laid eyes on him, and I am still drawn to him like a kid to candy. Part of me wants to say yes and never look back. But part of me can't. I draw his hand close to my heart. "I need some time to think."

He grins. "That's what you said about the concert, and look how awesome that turned out."

I smile. "True."

He lowers his voice to a near whisper. "If you need time, take it. I'll be here."

He leans toward me, and I close my eyes. His kiss is soft and smooth and easy. It's a lot like breathing.

And a little like choking.

Chapter
FORTY-THREE

Brie holds up a black-and-blue sweater and frowns. "Why are boys so hard to buy for?"

"Blake is not hard to buy for," Maggs says.

"Right?" I say. "Get him anything with a Nats logo and he'll love it."

"I got him a Nationals jersey last Christmas. And a jacket for his birthday. I need to mix it up this time."

I survey the sea of guys' clothing around me. Should I be buying a present for a boy this year? And if so, which one? I clear my throat. I have something I need to tell my friends. I've been putting it off because I know how they'll react. "So. About last night."

Brie and Maggs both drop the shirts they're holding and turn to me.

"Yeah?"

"What happened?"

"Ty kissed me. And said he wants to get back together."

Brie tenses up but says nothing.

Maggs pastes on a smile. "And what did you say?"

"I told him I needed some time to think, which I've been doing, but which does not seem to be working." I cover my face with my hands. "Seriously, I have no idea what to do."

Brie gives me a hug, which is unexpected but exactly what I need. Brie can surprise me that way.

"I made up a list of the pros and cons of dating Ty." I run through it for them, and there are so many pros, I run out of fingers. There's only one con, but he's a very big con.

I groan. "Why does this have to be so hard?"

"I don't know," Brie says. "Too bad there isn't some magic formula out there that can tell you what to do."

"Exactly," I say. "That's what I need."

Brie stares at me, smirking, waiting for me to get it.

When I finally do, I can't help but laugh. "Okay, very funny. So I guess that's two cons: Libby doesn't think Ty is my match."

"And Libby is never wrong."

I stick out my tongue. Speaking of Libby's matches, I turn to Maggs. "What about you?"

"Me? What about me?"

"I don't know. I sort of feel like … you and Aiden? There's maybe a spark there?"

She shrugs and busies herself with examining another sweater. "We may have bonded in the back seat as we tried to avoid gagging over you and Ty and your Factory Boys fandom." She attempts to imitate our singing and, of course, screws up the lyrics.

"Hashtag Assembly Line!" I say as I offer her a fist.

Maggs gives me a bump. "If I'm being honest, I do think he's kind of cute."

"You do?"

She nods. "It's the dark eyes. And that sweet smile—the way his top lip sort of goes … " She attempts a lopsided grin that looks more deranged than sweet. "Only his is cuter, obviously."

"Obviously." Brie takes the sweater from her and holds it up. "This seems like a winner. Blake looks hot in gray." She turns to me. "But *you* don't get to change the subject so easily. We need to figure out whether you're going to choose Ty or Darius. You can't go into Christmas break undecided."

She's right. I'd obsess over it. It would ruin my holiday. Besides, stringing along two boys is not my style.

"Want my advice?" Brie takes a step toward me and continues without waiting for my reply. "Here it is: You named a dozen pros of dating Ty and only one con. But if that one con is a match for all those pros—and since you're so tortured about this, I think it is—well … there's your answer. Your heart is telling you something, and it's time for your mind to start listening."

Chapter
FORTY-FOUR

I hate it when Brie's right. But, once again, she is. I've mulled it over all weekend. Ty comes with some amazing perks, but when I close my eyes, Darius is the boy I dream about.

I clutch a roll of paper towels to my chest and inhale the lemony scent of the F Hall janitor's closet. I texted Ty to meet me here before school starts so I can give him my answer. I want to do it in person, and I want to be as far away from our classmates as possible so we can avoid a scene.

It's not his reaction I'm worried about; it's my own. *Can I even do this? Will my mouth form the words necessary to tell Ty Walker I do not want to date him?*

I hear footsteps turning the corner to the hallway, so I sit down on a stool. Then I stand, then sit, then stand again. What should I be doing? Ty opens the door and catches me halfway between a sit and a stand, and I knock over the stool.

"Oh, hi."

He grins, eyebrows raised, and shuts the door behind him. It suddenly occurs to me that the F Hall janitor's closet may have been a poor choice. What if he has the wrong idea? I pick up the stool and perch on it and motion for him to take a seat on the stepladder next to me.

He gently takes the roll of paper towels away and sets them on a shelf behind us, and he takes my hands in his. "You're trembling."

"Am I? Maybe a little." My voice certainly is.

He scoots his ladder closer and wraps his arm around my waist. Okay, this is not going as planned. Part of me is tempted to switch gears and go with the flow. My body involuntarily leans into him, and it takes every ounce of mental scolding to pull it back. I jump up and practically knock over the stool again. "Sorry. I … the thing is … I … wanted to talk."

"Okay."

I pace back and forth in the closet. "I want to thank you for taking me to the concert—Maggs and Brie, too—and for the candy cane, and for asking me to get back together, but … " My voice cracks, and I stop. *What am I doing?*

Ty stands and walks toward me. He hands circle my hips. "There is no 'but.' We were good together, Alicea, and we can be again. We belong together."

I meet his gaze. Those are words I've believed with all my heart for years, and words I want to believe even now. But Libby says they're a lie. So did the choking sensation I had when he kissed me the other night. And so does the feeling I get whenever I think about Darius Groves.

I close my eyes and shake my head. "There *is* a 'but.' I

wish there weren't, but there is." I take a deep breath and pull him toward me, into a final hug, partly so he can't see the tears forming. I'm ending something that has been at the center of my dreams and desires since the start of high school. A month ago, this would have been unthinkable. "So thank you again, but … " My voice catches in my throat. "No. I can't."

We stand like that for a long minute. When the warning bell rings, Ty kisses the top of my forehead and leaves without a word. I grab a paper towel and press it to my face as I slump onto the stool. *I did it. I actually said "no."*

I can still feel the sensation of Ty's arms around me as we stood here, and a huge part of me would do anything to have that back, but I take a deep breath and picture Darius. Because he is my new "yes." And that thought makes so much sense to me in this moment, I know saying goodbye to Ty was right. It hurt, but it was right.

I blow my nose into the paper towel and force myself to stand. I wipe my eyes, stretch my shoulders back, and emerge into F Hall. As I walk through the school toward my locker, I give myself the mother of all pep talks.

You've got this, Alicea. You did what you had to do. You should be proud of yourself. You're not the same girl you were when you first saw Ty freshman year. You're not even the same person you were last year when you hired Lexi to whisper him. You're a brave, confident senior now, and you need to use that confidence to show the world that you don't care what anyone thinks. You and Darius Groves are a couple, and if they don't like it, that's their problem.

As I round the corner to face the crowds of C Hall, I

force a smile. A guy from my gym class smiles back. Two sophomores in cheer uniforms wave at me. As my smile gets wider and wider, a girl I swear I've never even seen before gives me a thumbs up. Can these people see the change in me? Have I finally found the swagger I envied in Ty so long ago?

I stop at my locker, and as I twirl the combination, I find myself humming the Factory Boys. *Your eyes, your lips, your sweet curvy lines. And in my dreams, I make you mine, so fine.*

"Well, aren't you in a good mood?"

I look up to find Lauren grinning at me. "I am, actually."

"You should be." She leans toward me, her eyes wide, her tone conspiratorial. "I knew you could do better. Way to go." And with that, she flounces off down the hallway.

My locker pops open and slams into my knee, but I barely feel it.

Way to go? What's that supposed to mean?

Chapter
FORTY-FIVE

I lean my head against the chain of the swing. It's rattling, and it takes me a while to realize it's because I'm shaking. Where's Darius? I texted him to meet me here after school. What if he doesn't show?

I pull up the photo on my phone for the millionth time today and stare. Ugh. Brie and Maggs and I had a deal Friday night. No Instagramming, for obvious reasons, but apparently Brie failed to inform Blake. This morning he posted a selfie from the concert with Brie, and there in the background, as clear as a bright spring day, are Ty and me dancing and laughing. One of Blake's friends tagged Ty, and the comments began pouring in, dozens of them, all assuming we'd kissed and made up and gotten back together.

When I discovered all of this shortly after the start of first period, I ran to the nurse's office, called my mom, and got permission to go home sick. It was only a partial lie. All day long I lay in bed wondering what I should say to Darius.

My phone beeps.

```
Brie: I am so sorry. Please text back.
```

It's her thousandth text of the day, but I can't bring myself to respond. This is a disaster. How could she be so careless?

I twist the swing around and around and around, lean back, and let it unwind as I peer up into the sky, wishing I could fly away into the clouds. As angry as I am at Brie, I know she's not really the one to blame. I close my eyes. *What have I done?*

"Hey." Darius's voice startles me. "I got your text."

I plant my feet on the ground and stand, dizzy from all the twirling. I grasp at the chain and try to meet his gaze, but he looks away.

"Thanks for coming. I was afraid you ... might not."

"Yeah, well." He clenches his jaw, and the scar on his chin appears darker than usual. "I wanted to be sure to congratulate you on getting back together with Wonder Boy. Guess you two deserve each other." With that, he looks me in the eye, a challenge hovering in his stare.

"We're not back together. Like I said in my text, it's all a big misunderstanding."

"A misunderstanding." His tone is as sharp as his gaze. "Which part? Did I misunderstand you when you told me you couldn't get together this weekend because you had too much Christmas stuff to do? Or did I misunderstand you when I texted to ask how your weekend was and you forgot to mention you went to a concert with Ty? Or maybe the part I misunderstood was the part where we spent the past three weeks here in this crappy little park making out and I thought we actually … " His voice gives out. "Whatever. I'm guessing it was all of the above."

"No." I walk toward him, but he backs off. For the millionth time today, my eyes well up. I can feel the hurt, the betrayal, emanating from him. It's a feeling I know too well and one I certainly never meant to inflict on him. "Can I please explain?"

Darius turns and walks away, and for a moment, I'm afraid he's leaving, but he stops and hoists himself up onto the center bar of the seesaw. He picks at a rust spot, silent.

I walk over and lift the seesaw, balancing it at its midpoint. I need something to hold onto, something to keep me from grabbing him as I so desperately want to do. "Yes, Ty and I went to the concert, but no, we are not back together." I tell him the whole story, from the candy cane right through to our goodbye hug this morning in the F Hall janitor's closet. I leave out the part about the kiss. "I'm sorry. I should have told you."

I wait for him to respond, but he sits, mute, pick-pick-picking at the rust.

I drop the seesaw and risk walking closer to him. "The thing about getting ready for Christmas was partly true, because I did go shopping Saturday and I baked two pies yesterday, not that that makes it right, but—"

"Come on, Alicea." His head snaps up, and his eyes meet mine. "You lied. Admit it."

I recoil at his words.

He stands to leave, but I grab his arm. "You're right," I say. "I lied. But that's only because I didn't want to hurt you."

"Oh, I see." His laugh is hard. "How's that working out for you?"

I shut my eyes. I deserve this. I know it. "I said I'm sorry, and I am. I don't know what else to do."

"I know what you should do."

I wait for it. *Is he going to tell me to get out of his sight? Go back to Ty? Go to hell?*

He leans toward me, and when he speaks, his voice is so soft I can barely hear him. "You should figure out why you were willing to give up your dream of dating Ty Walker to go out with a guy like me." With that, he shakes off my hold, turns, and walks across the playground to his car, leaving me to stare after him.

Well. That was unexpected.

Chapter
FORTY-SIX

I convince Mom and Dad to let me stay home from school the next day. It's Tuesday, the last day before Christmas break, and half my teachers are mailing it in with movies and games anyway. This gives me a full nine days before I have to face Darius, Ty, and hallways full of my classmates. With the exception of a few texts with Maggs and Brie, whom I've finally forgiven, I have zero contact with the outside world for three days.

The first time I venture outside the house is to go to church on Christmas Eve. Of course, the first hymn we sing is "Angels We Have Heard on High," and I spend the rest of the service trying not to cry. How could I have screwed things up with Darius so thoroughly?

As we leave the service, I hear someone calling my name. With the Christmas Eve crowd, I thought I might escape without having to talk to anyone from school. I turn to find Aiden heading toward me.

I force a smile. "Hey. I didn't know you went to St. James."

"We don't come very often. Christmas and Easter mostly." He leans toward me. "Can we talk?"

I nod to my brother. "Tell Mom and Dad I'll meet you at the car." I grab Aiden's arm and pull him off toward an empty alcove. "What's up?"

He digs around in his pocket. "I got a gift for Maggs." He opens a small rectangular box to reveal an orange leather wrap bracelet with daisy beads. "Think she'll like it?"

I stare, mouth open. It is *so* Maggs.

"It's too much, isn't it?" Aiden shoves the box back into his pocket, muttering, "I'm such an idiot. What am I thinking? Maggs barely knows I'm alive."

"She thinks you're cute." It's out before I can stop myself.

"What?"

I purse my lips. *Darn it.* Did I seriously just break the best friend code?

"Did she tell you that?"

"Maybe."

"What exactly did she say?"

"Nothing. I've revealed too much already. Still ... I think you should give her the bracelet. It's perfect. She'll love it."

"You think?"

"I do."

"Cool. I was planning to surprise her with it after your New Year's Eve performance."

"Perfect. And Aiden?"

"Yeah?"

"Be sure to flash that smile when you give it to her."

I barely sleep that night, and not because I'm excited for Santa. I keep turning Darius's question over in my mind. Why did I pick him over Ty? It wasn't just because of Libby, or the kissing, or even the way Darius makes me feel. There's more to it, but I can't quite put my finger on it. Of course, none of it matters now that I've blown it with him.

I groan into my pillow. A moment later, my bedroom door flies open.

"Are you okay?" It's Andrew.

"Don't you ever knock?" I sit up and blink hard, trying to erase all traces of Darius Groves from my brain. "I'm fine. Go away."

Andrew hesitates.

"What?"

He points to my tablet. "I guess you've seen it?"

"Seen what?"

He steps into my room and sits down at my desk. "It's not that bad, you know. In fact, I think it's kind of cool."

"What are you talking about?"

Andrew gives me a side-eye. "You really haven't seen it?"

"I don't know, since you haven't told me what it is."

"Oh, if you'd seen it, you'd know."

"Then tell me." I'm shouting now.

"Okay, okay." He holds up his hands. "Sorry. I thought I heard you moaning, so I figured … Joe Blackman sent me the link. It's a video. I don't think you're going to like it."

"A video? What the—?" An alarm bell goes off in my head. Joe graduated with Andrew. His sister, Lacy, is in my class. Whatever "it" is, if Joe has seen it, Lacy has probably seen it. And if Lacy has seen it, the entire school has seen it.

Andrew pulls out his phone. "Calm down. I'll send it to you."

I grab my phone and click on his text, and the video pops up. It's Darius's rap. My heart aches at the sight of his ocean blue eyes peering at me from my screen. "This is the video? I've seen this. It's no big—"

The words catch in my throat, because the sound track continues playing the rap, but the video suddenly changes. Instead of Darius dancing, it's me. Last year. At prom. I stare in horror as the camera zooms in and shows me perched atop a riser by the DJ's stage, eyes closed, twirling like a deranged dervish.

I was in my own world that night, reeling—literally—from the breakup with Ty. I'd wanted to skip prom, but I was up for queen, so everyone would have noticed. They would have assumed I was home sobbing into a giant bowl of ice cream. Pride made me go. I would not let Ty make a fool of me.

Instead, I made a fool of myself.

I have no idea what possessed me to climb up on that riser. I only know I wanted to shut out the rest of the world and lose myself in the music.

"No, no, no." My stomach clenches as I watch myself stomp and sway and perform dance moves I'd never even realized I could do. What a nightmare. I'd faced hallway stares and giggles for pretty much the rest of the school year. There had been at least a dozen videos going around, taken from every possible humiliating angle. Mercifully, the whole thing blew over during the summer. Until now. I guess Darius's video gave some idiot an excuse to dig up their footage and create this homage to my mortification.

Finally, as the rap ends, my image fades and the video switches back to Darius and the last line from our presentation. "Promposal, Shakespeare style." Crap. He's probably the one person at Grand View who'd never seen any of those videos. Guess he will now.

"I like how they matched up some of your movements with the song," Andrew says. "Like when he sings, 'Come off your cloud,' you're doing that thing where it sort of looks like your arms are floating, and then later, when—" His mouth snaps shut as he notices my glare. "Seriously. It's kind of cool."

I start to protest, but my phone buzzes. And buzzes again. Maggs. Then Brie. Oh, my. This is spreading quickly. "Out." I point to the door, and Andrew rises to go. He attempts to imitate my floating-arm motion, and I throw my pillow at him. "Stop. And shut the door behind you."

I clutch my phone, eyes closed, trying to calm my breathing before checking my texts. That photo with Ty and me already had everyone talking, and now this. It's too much.

```
Brie: You OK?
Maggs: Call me.
```

I text Brie back to tell her I'm fine, even though I'm not, and I call Maggs.

"Hey. I'm guessing you've seen it?"

"Yes. My life is over."

"No. It's fine. It's kind of cool, actually."

"That's what Andrew said, but it's not cool. It's horrifying." I sink back into my pillows and close my eyes.

"Who do you think made it?"

"Who knows? Probably someone who heard the rumors about Ty and me getting back together and wants to embarrass me. Could be one of his exes. Or girlfriend wannabes. I don't even want to know."

"Well, I wouldn't worry too much. By the time we go back to school, everyone will forget about it."

"Or not. It took two months for them to stop talking about it the first time."

"More like a month. And I know you refuse to believe it, but there were plenty of us who thought your dancing was really cool. And in the video, with Darius rapping, it's even cooler." She pauses. "Alicea?"

"Yeah?"

"How are you doing? Are you going to be okay?"

I sigh. "Probably not. I'm thinking about going emo. I'll wear lots of black, and eyeliner, and perma-earbuds so I can legit ignore everyone forever."

Maggs snorts. "You couldn't pull that off."

"I could."

"No. Sorry, babe, but you couldn't. Nor should you try. You should rock what you've got. You need to look everyone in the eye—including Ty and Darius—and act like you own the world."

"Right. Emo it is, then."

Maggs giggles. "Give it a few days. You'll come around. And Merry Christmas. "

"Thanks, Maggs. I feel a little better already." I do. Maggs has that effect on people.

Still, a little extra eyeliner never hurt anyone.

Chapter
FORTY-SEVEN

Turns out it's impossible to be emo and wear a tiara. I can't help but smile as I check every angle in the mirror. Tonight's the night. This week's rehearsals were rough, mainly because my feet—and my whole body, really—felt as though they were made of lead. I need to put my mood aside, forget about my miserable love life, and become Dewdrop. My stomach tightens. Can I pull it off?

Mom stops by my bedroom door. "Oh, sweetheart, you look beautiful."

I strike a pose. "You look pretty, too. I love the scarf."

She smiles and comes over to kiss me on the cheek. "Your dad and I are going to head over to the gallery now. We'll pop down to the studio at nine to watch." She starts to leave. "Do you think you'll be able to come up for a while? If you're too busy, we'll understand."

"Sure. I should be able to stop in during one of our breaks. Not that you'll need any warm bodies tonight." The gallery tends to get a big crowd for the First Night Celebration.

"Good." She grins. "We have a very special exhibit tonight. I think you'll enjoy it."

"Can't wait." I paste on a smile. Mom's idea of "special" and mine are very different. Whatever it is, I'm guessing it won't feature monarch butterflies.

I'm the first girl to arrive at the studio, and Ms. DuBois calls me into her office. I brace myself. She's been tough on me this week, and rightfully so. I take a seat on the bench, and before she can even shut the door, I try to explain. "Ms. DuBois, I know I screwed up a million times this week, and even when I wasn't screwing up, my dancing wasn't exactly inspired, but I promise that tonight—"

"Alicea." She holds up her hand to stop me. "I have no doubt you'll make me proud tonight. That is not why I asked you in here."

"Oh. Okay." I wait for her to elaborate, but she simply stares at me, as though trying to puzzle something out.

Finally, she reaches over to her desk and picks up her phone. "I called you in here because of this."

As she swipes at her screen, the realization hits. *O. M.*

G. How did that video get all the way to Ms. DuBois? Has everyone in the entire freaking county watched it?

Sure enough, she plays it for me.

"Yes. I've seen it." I motion for her to turn it off. "I'm sorry. I look ridiculous. I'm so embarrassed, and—"

"Stop." She frowns and folds her arms across her chest. "I don't want apologies."

I bite my lip. Wow. She is really upset. Why does she … oh, no. She wouldn't kick me out of dance, would she? And certainly not before tonight's performance? I know that video doesn't exactly represent DuBois Dance Studio in the best light, but that was prom. It was on my own time, and it would be totally unfair if—

"I think this is wonderful." She shakes the phone at me.

"What?"

"This is what I've been trying to get from you for months."

"You've been trying to get me to do … that?"

"Well, not this exactly, but … " She hits play again. "Look at this emotion, this passion."

I watch, but all I see is a girl making a fool of herself. I cringe and hit the "stop" button. I shake my head. "That right there is a mess."

"No." Ms. DuBois sits down next to me. "Not a mess. It's … raw. And sometimes raw is good." She takes my hands in hers. "Alicea, you are a skilled dancer. You practice so hard, you have beautiful technique, and you learn the choreography. You perform every movement just so. Sometimes, though, I wish you would … let go. Surrender. Like in the video."

"I understand," I say, even though I most certainly do

not. Ballet dancers do not "let go." They exercise discipline and precision. "I need to surrender. Of course."

I stand, and Ms. DuBois's eyes narrow. It seems as though she wants to say something more, but she simply sighs and motions me toward the door. "*Toi toi toi.*"

It's how Ms. DuBois wishes us luck before a performance. I feel as though tonight I'll need it.

Chapter FORTY-EIGHT

We've prepared four dances, and we're performing each of them twice throughout the night. In between, visitors can talk to the dancers and enjoy cider and cookies. We kick off at eight with the "Dance of the Sugar Plum Fairy." Afterward, while the other girls mingle, I hide out in the dressing room. I saw a few kids from my calc class in the audience. I don't want to deal with their stares and whispers, and I'm not in the mood to fake happy with everyone anyway.

"There you are." Brie appears in the doorway. "You okay?"

I nod. "I'm fine. I just … can't."

"I get it." She comes over and pulls me into a hug. "You'll to have to stay out there after the 'Waltz of the Flowers,' though. You know that, right? Everyone will want to talk to you."

I bury my face into her shoulder. "I know. But maybe no

one will come to it. Except my parents, and I can deal with them."

"Yeah, well, since about a hundred people showed up for this one, I wouldn't count on it."

I sigh. "A girl can dream."

She pulls away and holds me at arm's length. "Listen to me. You do not want an empty house for the 'Waltz.' You want everyone in Loudoun County to watch you rock your tiara as you jump and twirl among us mortal petunias."

"Petunias? I've always thought of you more as lilies."

"Really?" Brie cocks her head as though considering this. "Lilies do seem more dignified. I think I can work with that." She shakes her head, and her tone becomes serious. "Anyway, here's the thing: I personally think that video of you dancing is awesome, but if you hate it so much, you should look at this as your chance to redeem yourself. Show the world what you've got."

I nod and force a smile. "Thanks, Brie. I appreciate the pep talk, but—"

"No buts. You're going to make a fabulous Dewdrop, and that's all anyone needs to know. You go out there, you leave everything you have on that dance floor, and … bam. Drop the mic."

I grin. "Could you imagine Ms. DuBois's face if I actually mimed a mic drop at the end?"

We both crack up.

"Speaking of Ms. DuBois," Brie says, "she's going to wonder where we are. We should go back out."

I motion for her to leave. "Go ahead. I just need a few more minutes."

Brie gives me another quick hug and heads to the door.

"And Brie?"

She turns around.

"Thanks."

"Of course. That's what friends are for."

As she leaves, I sink onto a bench. Maybe Brie is right. Perhaps a strong performance tonight could help me redeem myself with my classmates.

Now if only I could figure out how to redeem myself with Darius.

Our eight-thirty performance of the "Waltz of the Snowflakes" goes without a hitch, and I even force myself to stick around for a few minutes afterward to meet and greet. Coming up next is the "Waltz of the Flowers," and the butterflies have taken flight. As I grab a glass of cider to help calm my stomach, I spot two girls coming in the front door. Oh, no. Lauren and Michelle. Seriously? I can't deal with them right now.

"Ms. DuBois?" I interrupt her conversation with one of the parents. "I'm sorry. Can I run upstairs to the gallery? I told my mom I'd make an appearance."

She glances at the clock. "I think that would be a mistake. The 'Waltz' is in twenty minutes."

"Please. I'll make it super quick."

She nods and waves her hand. "Do not be late for the 'Waltz.'"

I take off and scoot out the back entrance. I head up and open the door to the gallery to find my mom beaming in the lobby, which is buzzing with people.

"Hello, dear." She waves me over. "How's the dancing going?"

"So far so good. The 'Waltz' is next, so I only have a few minutes."

She nods. "We haven't forgotten. Andrew said he'll take over for your dad and me at nine so we can watch. And he'll come down at eleven to see the second performance." She flashes a conspiratorial smile. "Ready to check out that exhibit I was telling you about?"

I shrug. "Sure."

She leads me down a hallway toward one of the alcoves usually reserved for student art. As we walk, it dawns on me. *Oh, crap. Darius.* His mixed media piece. How could I have forgotten? I stop. "Is this what I think it is?"

"That depends on what you think it is."

"Come on, Mom." I hadn't exactly advertised to my family that Darius and I were dating—or whatever it is we were doing—but I'm pretty sure they picked up on the fact that we were texting and hanging out a lot. "You know what I'm thinking."

"In that case, yes, that's exactly what it is. And I think you'll really—" Her grin disappears as I start to back away. "Sweetheart, what's wrong?"

"Nothing. I should get back downstairs."

"But … " Her eyes widen. "Oh, no. Did you two have a fight?"

I nod. "Sort of. Not so much a fight as a—" Footsteps sound behind me, and I turn to find Darius walking down the hallway toward us. *Fabulous.* My stomach lurches, and the cider from earlier threatens to come up. I train my eyes on the floor and rush past him.

Ms. DuBois was right. This *was* a huge mistake.

Chapter
FORTY-NINE

The "Waltz of the Flowers" is a blur. Thankfully, I've practiced it a million times, and muscle memory takes over. The pace of the waltz—at times calm and at times frenetic—feels like a crescendo of my week's emotions. I allow myself to get lost in the music until it's just me and Tchaikovsky and the smooth, hard floorboards beneath my feet.

With my body on autopilot, my *pliés* feel somehow too deep, my *relevés* almost bouncy, and my *pirouettes* too loose. I'm a mess, but at least I manage to get through my solo without tripping or trampling any of the other dancers or, worse, bursting into tears. Afterward, I try to make an escape to the dressing rooms, but Maggs and Brie both tackle me.

"That was awesome."

"Great job."

"Not really," I say.

"Yes, really." Maggs is beaming. "You were amazing."

"I was?"

"You were." Brie mimics a mic drop.

Ms. DuBois approaches us and favors me with a small smile. "Nicely done, Alicea." She motions toward the front of the studio. "And now, your adoring fans await."

I take a deep breath and force a smile. Okay, so maybe it wasn't so bad. But I still don't want to go out there. I consider asking whether I can skip the mingling, but the look in Ms. DuBois's eyes tells me resistance is futile. I have to do this.

I fidget with my tiara as I head toward the front of the studio and make my way into the crowd. My mother immediately gathers me up into a hug. "Lovely dancing. Simply lovely."

Dad hands me a bouquet of pink roses. "Congratulations. You did it."

"Thanks, Mom. Thanks, Dad." I relax a bit, and my smile broadens. "These are beautiful."

I accept hugs and air kisses from Maggs's parents, Brie's mom, one of my teachers from sixth grade, and a few of the younger dancers. This isn't so bad. If anyone else tells me how awesome I was, I might not even need to fake—

I blink. What the … ? Darius and Jaycee are standing by the cookie table, watching me. Jaycee jumps up and down and smiles and waves. I offer them a small nod. What is he thinking? Why would he do this to me?

I walk toward them, a newly formed knot in my stomach tightening with each step. "Hi, there."

Jaycee gives me a hug. "Cool tiara."

"I know, right?" I risk a glance at Darius, but he's engrossed in pouring himself a cup of cider. "Thanks for coming."

"Darius didn't even tell me you were dancing, so I didn't know until I saw the program. I came out tonight mostly for the friendship bracelet workshop at the jewelry store next door. Well, that and my brother's paintings."

"Mixed media." It's the first words Darius has spoken, or more accurately, mumbled.

"Pardon me." Jaycee rolls her eyes. "Mixed media." She grabs my hand. "Have you seen them yet?"

"Them? So there's more than one?" I direct this at Darius, but he continues to avoid my gaze.

"There are three." Jaycee is bouncing again. "But they're all related. One of them is—"

"All right, Jay." Darius sets his cup down on the table. "Enough chatter. We need to get going."

"Going where? We already did the bracelets, and you said the only other thing you cared about was the dancing, so—"

"Enough." He grabs her coat sleeve, but she pulls away and waves at someone across the room.

"There's Netta. I'm going to go say hi to her." And with that, she takes off, leaving us alone together at the cookie table. Not at *all* awkward.

"Great job up there. With the dancing." For the first time, Darius looks up at me, and the hurt in his eyes sends a pang of regret through my heart.

I hate that I caused that pain. Is there anything I can do to take it away? Jaycee said it was his idea to come see the "Waltz." Does that mean it's not too late? I gather up a shock of tulle from my skirt and smooth it in my hand. "Thank you. And thanks for coming. It means a lot to me." He says nothing, so I force myself to go on. "I know I screwed up. I can't believe I messed up something so amazing, and I know you don't owe me anything, and I don't actually expect you to forgive me, but I hope you'll at least accept my apology. Because I'm sorry. I am really, truly sorry."

Darius's eyes soften ever so slightly, and he nods. "Apology accepted." He walks toward me, and for one wonderful, horrible moment, I think he's going to kiss me, but he stops and tosses his cup in the garbage can.

He glances around and takes another step toward me. His lowers his head so that his lips are just inches from mine. I drop the tulle. As much as I want to close the gap between us and kiss him, I know I've lost the right to do that.

"Know what you reminded me of up there?" he asks.

I shake my head because I don't trust my voice.

"A butterfly. The way you kind of … floated."

"Me? Float?"

"Yeah. And you know what they say."

"What's that?"

"Float like a butterfly, sting like a bee." And with that, he crosses the room, wrangles Jaycee, and walks out into the night.

Ouch.

Chapter
FIFTY

After our last dance of the evening, we all pull on our coats and scarves to go out to the courthouse. This is my favorite part of First Night, when all the performers—musicians, artists, dancers, actors, puppeteers—gather with the spectators and shopkeepers at the courthouse by candlelight to count down to midnight.

I spot Mom, Dad, and Andrew by the courthouse wall and make my way over.

Andrew gives me a thumbs-up. "Nice job tonight, Al."

"Thanks." Our second performance of the "Waltz" was not as successful as the first, judging from Ms. DuBois's reaction, but we got through it without any major mistakes.

"There was one part I didn't quite get," Andrew says.

"Didn't get?"

"Yeah. When you were doing your spins—"

"*Foettés*."

"Whatever. All the other dancers were slowly moving toward the back of the stage."

"I wondered about that too," my mom says. "Did that signify isolation or veneration? It was a bit confusing."

I roll my eyes. "I'm pretty sure Ms. DuBois just choreographed it that way so that if I started to lose my balance, I wouldn't kick anyone."

Mom and Andrew laugh, but I can tell they're not convinced. Everything has to have a deeper meaning with those two. I decide to change the subject. "So how did everything go tonight at the gallery?"

"Oh, it was wonderful." My mom clasps her hands together. "We had our biggest crowd yet. And we sold almost every piece in the student show."

"Really? That's amazing." I force a smile. Does that mean they sold Darius's pieces? My stomach sinks. I'd waited so long to see his artwork, but tonight, when I had the chance, I ran away. What if I never get to see them? I turn to my father. "Hey, Dad, I need to use the bathroom. Can you give me the key to the gallery?"

Dad pulls his keys out of his pocket and hands them to me. I snatch them and take off across the street, into the arts building, and upstairs to the gallery. Please, please let Darius's exhibit still be here.

I rush down the hallway toward the student art alcove. I round the corner, and—*whoa*. I catch my breath. Displayed at the center of the alcove are three canvases on easels. Each depicts an angel—one surrounded by a swarm of monarch butterflies, one wearing a leotard and skirt in a classic *arabesque* pose, and one balancing atop a perfectly symmetrical snowflake. The pieces are all very different, but their ethereal vibe and the identical haloes gracing the crowns of the angels tie them all together. They're made from a medley of magazine clippings, tissue paper, cloth, paint, and what appears to be wood shavings. "Wow."

"You like them?"

I turn around with a shriek.

"Sorry." Darius raises his hands in apology. "I didn't mean to scare you. I saw you running up here, so I followed you."

"I thought you went home."

"I took Jay home and came back. You know, you really should have locked the door behind you. What if someone had followed you in here? I mean, someone besides me."

"You're right. I should have, but I was kind of in a hurry, and … " I turn and point to his artwork. "These are amazing."

"Thank you. I had an amazing subject."

My heart skips a beat, and I can't help but smile despite the tears that have sprung to my eyes. I was once his angel bright. Someone he cared about enough to create these. His muse, as my mother would say. Who would ever have imagined I, Alicea Springer, could be someone's muse? Perhaps that's what it means to be someone's perfect match.

"Can I ask you something?"

"Sure."

"This might seem like a weird question, but … " I hesitate. It is a very odd question, but I feel like I need to know his answer. "Tonight, in the 'Waltz,' when I was doing the *foetté* spins and the other dancers were creeping toward the back of the stage, what do you think that signified?"

"What do you mean?"

"I'm sorry. This is silly. You probably don't even remember."

"No, I remember. Those were some impressive spins."

"But why do you think the other dancers moved away?"

He gazes into the distance as though considering this. "I don't know. I think maybe sometimes the 'Waltz of the Flowers' is just about flowers waltzing. I'm not sure it needs to mean more than that."

I grin. "Oh my gosh, thank you. That is so perfect."

He looks confused, but he laughs. "Okay."

"Can I ask you another question?"

"Go ahead."

I point to his artwork. "Why are these still here?"

"What do you mean?"

"My mom said most of the student artwork sold. Why not these? They're some of the most beautiful student pieces she's ever shown."

Darius reaches past me and points to a small sign in a bracket below one of the easels: ANGEL BRIGHT: NOT FOR SALE.

"That's why," he says. "They're a gift. For you."

I gasp. "What? No. I can't accept them."

"Please." He places his hand on the small of my back. "I want you to have them."

His touch sends a thrill through me, and I turn to meet his gaze. "Thank you." My voice comes out as barely more than a whisper. "Darius?"

"Yes?"

"I know you said you accepted my apology, but ... do

you think you can ever forgive me?" I feel myself shaking as I wait for his reply. I wouldn't blame him if he said no, or if he simply turned and walked away, and for a long moment, I fear he might.

Instead, he pulls me toward him into a kiss that takes my breath away. It's hard at first, but it mellows into the crazy, mind-jumbling, thought-erasing, whole-body-tingling kiss I know and love and can totally lose myself in.

It takes me a while to realize the explosions and cheers I'm hearing aren't all in my head. I pull away with a laugh, grab his hand, and pull him toward a window facing the courthouse, where the crowd has erupted into a raucous edition of "Auld Lang Syne," with fireworks bursting overhead.

"Happy New Year," I say.

"Happy New Year."

I pull him down for another kiss. *Perfection.* Surely nothing could go wrong after ringing in the year with a kiss like this.

Chapter
FIFTY-ONE

Things do go wrong, of course, two days later when school starts back. The gossip machine is in high gear. Every time I turn around, I hear Darius's rap coming from someone's phone, and when I walk into PE during third period, I catch Bailey Ingraham imitating one of my weirder dance moves.

But none of that matters. What matters is that Darius and I are back together. I don't care what other people are saying about me and Ty, or me and Darius, or me and that stupid dance.

"I'm telling you, it's cool. Especially with the rap." Maggs is playing it across the lunch table from me and keeping time—tap-tap-tapping her plastic yogurt spoon against the table—and bobbing her head to the music.

Brie joins in. "It's true. I don't know why you can't see it."

"I can't see it because I refuse to watch it because it's horrifying."

"What does Darius think about it?" Maggs asks.

"I have no idea."

"What do you mean?"

"We haven't talked about it. I can't. It's too embarrassing."

"I'm so glad you two are back together." Brie grins at me. "I'll bet he loves it. Because he sees what we see. Which is you, being awesome."

"Speaking of things that are awesome." I reach over and tug at Maggs's daisy-bead bracelet. "Where'd you get this? Super cute."

She blushes, a rare occurrence for Maggs, but she simply shrugs. "It was a Christmas present. You really like it?"

"It's adorable." I shoot Brie a look.

"Did your mom pick it out?" Brie's tone is so innocent, even I almost believe she has no idea who gave Maggs the bracelet, and I'm the one who told her.

"No." Maggs puts her hands over her face. "It was from a secret admirer."

"What? Are you serious?"

"How did you not tell us you have a secret admirer?"

Brie and I look at each other, incredulous. Did Aiden send it to her anonymously, or is she being coy?

"I'm telling you now." She leans forward, her voice low. "Someone left it on top of my ballet shoes on New Year's, after we went over to the courthouse. The tag had my name on it and said it was from a secret admirer."

"That's crazy." Brie clasps her hands together. "And so romantic. I repeat. Why are we just now finding out about this?"

Maggs covers her face again and squirms. "I don't know. I guess didn't say anything because I'm sort of … I mean … I have someone I want it to be." She squeals. "What if it's not him? It has to be him. But what if it's not?"

"Who do you want it to be?" I pry one of her fingers away from her face. "Maybe we can find out for you."

"No. I'm not ready to tell you guys yet."

"Can we try to guess?"

"No."

"Can you give us a hint?"

"No."

"Is he a senior?"

"Does he play a sport?"

"Stop. I'm not telling you, and I'm not giving out any hints. Not yet."

I sigh and finger one of the beads. "Well, whether this is from your mystery crush or not, it's perfect. Whoever gave it to you deserves a shot."

Maggs finally takes her hands away from her face and admires the bracelet. "It is perfect. Especially if it's from him."

Chapter
FIFTY-TWO

I turn the block over and over in my hand and read the letters out loud. "A. R. N. O. S. B. This has to mean something."

"Nah. It's a red herring," Darius says.

"A red herring?" Jaycee takes the block from me and looks at it. "What does that mean?"

"A red herring is something they plant in here to throw you off from the real clues."

We're locked in an escape room—a simulated classroom detention—and all of the puzzles so far have had an elementary school theme. We opened three of the five locks within the first half-hour, but since then we've been stuck.

On the wall next to me is a chart with dozens of brightly colored dots along with some simple math formulas:

Red + Blue =

Green – Yellow =
Orange – Red =
Purple – Blue =

Presumably the four answers will be the numbers we need to open the combination lock on the safe next to the chart. Problem is, I added and subtracted all the colored dots just like the formula says twice and tried every combination of the four numbers and came up with nothing. Which is why I've decided to move on to the block.

Darius walks over, and Jaycee hands it to him. He tosses it in the air, catches it, and spins one corner of it on his fingertip. "Oh, now I see."

"What?" Jaycee and I ask him in unison.

"B. A. R. N. O. S. Duh."

"Ha. Ha." I stick my tongue out.

Jaycee punches his arm and heads over to a bookcase in a far corner to search for more clues.

Darius puts his hand on my hip, and I half wish we could end up locked in here forever. Minus his sister and the spy cams.

"Should we ask them for a hint?" I ask.

"No. Not yet." Darius is very anti-hint.

I look around. "Have we opened these yet?" I walk over to the teacher's desk and begin opening the drawers. Inside one is a flashlight. "Interesting." I switch it on. "Hey. It's black light."

Jaycee runs over, and I hand it to her. She rushes around the room, shining it on every surface, until she stops and grins. "This is it!" She picks up a sheet of paper and brings it over to us. It has a series of partial words written in invisible ink:

Y E _ _
A _ E
W A _
B _ R _

"What the heck?" Jaycee cocks her head to one side. "YELL APE WAR BIRD?"

Darius and I laugh, but neither of us has a better guess.

"Wait a minute." I give Darius a triumphant stare as I slowly reach for the block. "Look. There are six missing letters. I'll bet these are them."

Together we try a few combinations until at last we piece it together: YEAR ABE WAS BORN.

"That has to be it. Do you happen to know when Abe Lincoln was born?"

Darius shakes his head. "Eighteen something?"

"Great. So we'll just try all the combinations starting with eighteen. That should only take about two hours."

"Oh, wait." Jaycee jumps up. "I think I saw something … " She rushes over to the bookcase and returns with a book called *Honest Abe*. She flips to the first page, and sure enough, it starts with, "Honest Abe Lincoln was born on February 12, 1809."

"Cool." Darius grabs one of the two combination-lock safes we have not yet opened and tries it, and *pop!* It opens up to reveal one of the keys we need to escape.

After high-fives all around, we turn our attention once again to the colored-dot puzzle.

"This is our last one," Darius says. "The only thing standing between us and recess."

"I feel like we're missing something," I say. "Just adding and subtracting all the dots is too easy. There must be some other—"

"Aha!" Darius jumps up and runs his hands through his hair. "It's so obvious."

"What is?"

Darius points at the puzzle. "This isn't about math class. It's about art class."

I squint and stare again at the dots, and finally it occurs to me. "Oooh. So red plus blue equals purple."

"So we count up the purple dots!" Jaycee gets to work figuring out the combination using our new formulas, and with almost two minutes to spare, we retrieve our final key and escape.

"We are free! We are free!" Jaycee bounces out the door and down the hallway.

"Nice work, Sherlock." I stop Darius, taking his hand in mine.

"You too."

"If I ever have to be stuck in detention, I want it to be with you."

"That's my kind of detention." Darius wriggles his eyebrows at me. "I think it's time to take Jaycee home."

Chapter FIFTY-THREE

After dropping Jaycee off, we head over to a party at Jack Baldwin's. I'm a little nervous. This is the first time Darius and I have shown up together anywhere, unless you count a basketball game, and that was with Jaycee. People could only be so rude when you have a ten-year-old kid sister with you. But tonight … this could be a disaster.

The first person I see when we walk through the door is Ty and two girls from the swim team who are fawning over him. I turn away, not because I can't bear to see him with those girls but because I don't want Darius to catch me watching him.

"Hi, Alicea." It's Lauren, and her sidekick, Michelle, is right behind her. "Hello, Darius." Her voice drips with disdain.

"Lauren." I wish I could smack the smirk off her face.

"So you two are official?"

I throw Darius a bemused look. "Apparently this matters to people." I sound a lot more confident than I feel as I glare at Lauren. "Guess I'd better change my Facebook status."

She sniffs. "No need for sarcasm."

"Also no need to explain myself to you." I grab Darius's hand and pull him past them, my heart racing. *Did I seriously just do that?* I hold up a hand and fist bump a random classmate as we make our way through the living room. That was pretty awesome, if I do say so myself. Maybe instead of a disaster, tonight will be one of the best—

My elation disappears as we round the corner into the kitchen, because standing by the refrigerator, laughing and flirting, is Maggs. With Milo. No, no, no. *This can't be.*

"Hey, you two." I sound perhaps a bit too cheerful. "What's going on?"

Maggs turns and gives me a hug. "You made it! How was the escape room?"

"Really fun. We got out with two minutes to spare."

"I want to try one of those sometime." She turns to Milo. "Have you ever done one?" I notice she plays with her bracelet as Milo regales us with a tale of his daring escape from a space station under attack by rebel forces at the Herndon Escape Room.

Ugh. I pull Darius aside. "I'll be right back. There's someone I need to talk to."

I search the house—the upstairs, the downstairs, the deck, the garage—and finally locate Aiden sitting alone on top of the dryer in the basement laundry room. "What are you doing here?"

"Good question. I shouldn't have come."

"No. I don't mean the party. I mean the laundry room. You need to be in the kitchen, talking to Maggs."

"I can't. It's no use. She'll never date a guy like me."

"What are you talking about? I told you, she thinks you're cute. And sweet. And she loves that bracelet, though you definitely should have put your name on the package. Secret admirer? What was that about?"

"I know. I'm an idiot. I had everything planned out that night. I was going to go up after your last dance and hand it to her and say something about her being the prettiest flower on the stage, and then … I wimped out. Couldn't do it."

I pull myself up onto the dryer beside him. "Listen. You're going to need to put yourself out there. Maggs likes you. I can tell she does. She just doesn't quite realize it yet."

"Yeah, well, there's one big thing standing between me and her."

"What?"

He looks at me like I'm dense. "Milo. That dude has way more game than me. And is about twice my size and has no problem at all getting up the nerve to talk to Maggs."

I give a dismissive wave. "Milo is … well, okay, Milo's pretty cute. But you have one thing going for you that he does not."

"What's that?"

"Libby. She says you and Maggs are a match. And that's not nothing."

Aiden cracks a small smile. "That's true."

I jump off the dryer and grab his arm. "Come on. Let's go. I got this." I pull out my phone and do a quick search as we head toward the kitchen. Please, please let my idea … *yes*. I grin. This is going to work. As we approach Maggs and Milo, I say in a loud voice, "Wow, that's cool. Maggs is going to be so excited."

Aiden shoots me a look that's half curiosity, half terror.

"About what?" Maggs turns to us.

"Tell her, Aiden."

Aiden's eyes widen.

"Oh, fine. I'll tell her." I pull at Maggs's arm, mostly in the hopes of creating some separation between her and Milo. "Did you know Phish is touring this summer? Aiden has an in. He's getting front-row seats."

Now Aiden's expression is half admiration, half terror. Whatever. He's got six months to figure out how to get the tickets.

"Are you serious?" Maggs claps her hands together. "I am so jealous. I am dying to see them."

"Who's Fish?" Milo looks lost.

"Only my favorite band ever. They were big in, like, the nineties and two thousands, but they're still together. They're kind of rock, kind of folk, kind of psychedelic … it's hard to explain."

I nudge Aiden, and he finally finds his voice. "Have you ever seen the video of them on Letterman?"

"The one where they played on top of the marquee? Oh my gosh, that was crazy."

Aiden nods. "They sounded so good. And then when they played 'Heavy Things' … "

"Yes! That's my favorite. I also love 'Billy Breathes,' though that one's kind of obvious."

"I need to go find Darius." I say this to no one in particular, because Maggs and Aiden are now uber focused on their Phish conversation, and Milo looks as though he desperately wants to find a way in but isn't even sure whether he's at the right address.

I locate Darius on the couch in the living room and cuddle up next to him. "Sorry about that. I had some business to take care of."

He puts his arm around me. "No worries."

I give him a kiss. Yes, there are people around and, yes, they can see us. And no, I don't care. Well, maybe I care a little bit. But not enough to stop me from kissing him. This is the new Alicea Springer, the one who in the space of less than an hour has dissed Lauren Cooke and come up with a sick plan to help Aiden get Maggs's attention. Nothing can—

Oh. My. Gosh. Am I hearing what I think I'm hearing? For real? I pull away from Darius to sit up and listen. Sure enough, someone is playing his rap. I glance around, and everyone in the room is either staring at us or trying desperately not to stare, and most of them are giggling. Whoever is playing the video turns up the volume, and several people start laughing out loud.

My face burns. I refuse to look at Darius. I scramble up from the couch and take off out of the living room, through the kitchen, down the basement steps, and into the laundry room.

Chapter
FIFTY-FOUR

I shouldn't have run. I should have summoned up the same courage I had earlier and laughed along with them. Heck, I should have jumped up and imitated my own dance moves and made fun of myself. After all, they can't laugh *at* me when they're laughing *with* me. It's just that everything about that night and that whole week was so awful. Seeing it played out over and over, with everyone making fun of me, brings it all back.

A knock sounds on the laundry room door, and Darius peeks in. "You okay?"

"Not really." I scoot over and make room for him on the dryer. "So I'm sure you've figured out by now that that was prom night, and it was just a few days after Ty broke it off with me." I bury my head in my hands. "I basically lost it. I don't remember much because I was so out of it. You must think I'm an idiot."

Darius puts his arm around me and pulls me into him. "Honestly, I think seeing the video helped."

I look up at him. "Helped? How?"

"Until I saw it, I didn't really get the whole thing with Wonder Boy. I mean, I knew you two had dated and I could tell you were still pretty hung up on him, but I guess ... " He stops, and the scar on his chin throbs. He looks away.

"What?"

"This is going to make me sound like a jerk, but ... I didn't realize how much he meant to you. I thought it was about you wanting to be 'Ty's Girlfriend.'" He makes air quotes. "I didn't stop to think that maybe you actually cared about him."

I take his hand in mine. "If I'm being honest, it was a little bit of both. I liked Ty. I liked him a lot. But I also liked the whole Look-at-Me-I'm-Ty's-Girlfriend thing."

We sit for a few minutes without saying a word. I wish we could stay here all night, tucked away, holding hands. When I finally dare to speak, I choose my words carefully. "I've thought about what you asked me that day in the park, about why I would give up my dreams of dating Ty to be with you."

"Oh, yeah?" He pulls away and faces me. "And did you figure it out?"

I tuck one leg up under me and turn to face him. "With Ty, I was the girl he picked to date out of all the other girls in the school, which made me feel special. But with you ... " I entwine my fingers in his. "With you, it's like there are no other girls. Or at least, the other girls don't matter." I pause and shake my head. "I'm not saying this right, but ... it's like no one else matters. It's just you and me, and all that … " I point to the ceiling "… stuff up there is white noise. I can ignore it and enjoy being me."

Darius grins. "My Angel Bright."

I feel myself blush. "I love it when you call me that."

"You didn't always."

"No. That's true. That's because at first, I have to admit, I … I refused to believe it."

"Believe what?"

"That Libby was right about our match."

Darius cocks his head. "What?"

I feel my cheeks grow warm. This is the first time I've acknowledged our Boyfriend Whisperer match. "I'm sorry, but when I first saw your name come up on my phone, I thought there was no way. I mean, Libby's never wrong, but … it seemed crazy to me."

Darius hops off the dryer and faces me. "What are you talking about? Who's Libby?"

"You know. My program. When you log on, it says, 'Hello, my name is Libby, and I'm here to help you find your perfect match.'"

"So the Boyfriend Whisperer thing? But what does that have to do with us?"

"What do you mean? It has everything to do with us. You're my match, and I'm yours. Libby says so."

He shakes his head. "Sorry if I'm being dense, but I don't get it. How does she know we're a match?"

I stare at him. Is he kidding? It's not that complicated. "Because of the survey. Our answers. She calculates them and … what's not to get?"

Darius says nothing, but I can tell he's as confused as ever.

I grip the edge of the dryer. Something's off. "What did you think all the questions were for? And why did you answer them if you weren't expecting to find a match?"

Darius opens his mouth, but nothing comes out.

"Oh, no." I get a cold, hard feeling in the pit of my stomach as the realization creeps in. "You didn't take the survey, did you? You've never used the Boyfriend Whisperer."

Chapter
FIFTY-FIVE

"**Y**ou have no idea what I'm talking about, do you?"

Darius shifts uncomfortably. "I mean, I know what the Boyfriend Whisperer is."

"But you've never even logged on."

"No. But I can if you want me to. What's going on? Why are you so upset?"

I'm shaking, and I feel as though I can't breathe. I can't believe this. Who would ... ? "Brie. Of course."

"What about Brie?"

"She created a fake account under your name and answered all the questions the way I would so we'd be matched."

Darius stares at me for a moment. "She did?"

"I'm sure of it."

He whistles. "Wow. That's some next-level matchmaking."

"This whole thing makes so much sense now. I can't

believe I didn't figure it out sooner." I jump off the dryer and stand beside him. "You're not my match after all. You never were."

"Well, but—"

"So what was with the winking and the pencil and the volunteering to be my Romeo and the … " My voice cracks. "The pinkie kiss?"

Darius shakes his head. "What do you mean, what was it? I did all that because I like you. Obviously."

"But why?"

"I don't know. Because I do. And I thought you liked me too." He looks away. "Who knew it was all a stupid computer program?"

I don't know what to say. Part of me wants to assure him it was more than that, but part of me isn't so sure. Because the fact is, if it hadn't been for Libby, I never would have given a guy like Darius Groves a chance.

"Libby's not stupid," I say finally, my voice barely a whisper. "In fact, she's never wrong." And with that, I turn and walk back upstairs, through the crowd and out the door.

I trace my fingers along the outline of one of the haloes. They don't shine as brightly here in my room, without the gallery lighting. For the past two weeks, ever since Darius gave these to me and we got back together, I've been trying to decide which "Angel Bright" piece is my favorite. It changes every day.

This morning, though, I have no favorite, because it turns out that none of the angels are real. They're all figments of my imagination, foolish wisps and dreams.

The doorbell rings, and I hear my mom answer. It's Brie. I've been expecting her. I texted her to come over this morning, though I didn't say why.

"Hey, there." She appears, smiling, in my doorway. "Wow, those really are gorgeous." She walks over to admire the canvases. "The pictures from your phone don't do them justice."

I sit down on my bed.

She turns to face me, and her smile disappears. "Are you okay? You look like you've been crying."

"How could you?"

Guilt flickers in her eyes ever so briefly, but she recovers. "How could I what?"

"Don't play dumb. Just tell me. Was the whole thing a plot to keep me away from Ty? And if so, couldn't you think of a better plan than to set me up with someone you knew I had no business dating?"

"What? Alicea, that's—"

"I can't believe I've been so dumb. There were about eight million signs that Darius and I did not belong together, but I chose to ignore all of them. I kept telling myself ... " I point an accusatory finger. "No, *you* kept telling me, 'Libby is never wrong,' and so I looked past all the red flags and let myself get caught up in something I knew from the beginning was stupid and ridiculous and would no doubt end badly. Which it did. Last night."

Brie's eyes widen. "Oh, no. What happened?"

"What happened? I figured out that you screwed me over and that the last two and a half months with him have been based on a great big lie, that's what happened."

She sits down at my desk chair. "Screwed you over? Alicea, that's not what I was doing. I was trying to help. And I kind of feel like it—"

"Want to hear the worst part? I came home last night and deleted your fake Darius account, and guess who my next closest match is? Yep. Ty. Seventy-four percent. Not perfect, but still. At least it's real."

"I'm sorry. I swear I didn't do it to hurt you. I hated seeing you so crazy after Ty. I thought it might help if you found someone else."

"I'm sure you did. You never thought I was good enough for him."

"Not good enough?" She moves onto the bed next to me. "Alicea, that's not true at all. I think you're too good for him. You deserve way better."

"Ha. Right. And so you set me up with some random new kid who was a known troublemaker with no friends. Because that's so much better."

"Yes, it is. Because Darius really likes you. I could tell he had a crush on you. And I think he's cute, and also funny, in a walls-up sort of way."

I glare. I don't want to think about how cute or funny Darius is right now. I've been trying, mostly unsuccessfully, to put him out of my mind all night.

"Come on, Alicea. He's into you, and you're into him, too. I know you are. What does it matter what Libby says?"

My jaw hardens. "Of course it matters."

"But why?"

"Because it does." *Doesn't it?* I hug my knees to my chest, and the tears start. Brie pulls me close into a hug, and even though I'm still mad at her, I let her.

After a long while, she pulls away and walks over to my desk to grab my box of tissues. "What did Maggs say about all this?"

"She doesn't know yet." I blow my nose. "I didn't want to mess things up with her last night. She was caught up in a conversation with Aiden—who *is* her match. For real." I can't help but throw that in. "So I didn't tell her. I called Andrew to come pick me up from the party and got the heck out of there." A thought occurs to me. "Did Maggs know anything about … ?"

"No. She never would have gone for it. This was all my idea. Here." Brie holds out her hand and takes my snot-filled tissues and tosses them in my trashcan. "Think you'll ever forgive me?"

"Maybe when we're old and gray."

"But I'm planning to color my hair until I die."

"Then no."

"That's what I thought." Brie gives me another hug. "I'm sorry you're upset, but honestly, I'm not sorry for setting you up. I one hundred percent believe you and Darius belong together, because first of all, every time you talk about him your whole face gets happy, and second … " She turns and points to the "Angel Bright" canvases. "He made those. I'd think the world was about to end if Blake ever did anything half that romantic for me."

I feel the tears start again and grab the tissue box. "I think you should go."

Brie sighs. "I'm going. But think about it. Because third of all, those tears are telling you something."

Chapter
FIFTY-SIX

"Tell me about Libby." Mrs. Barkley scans my poster, a smile playing at her lips. I'm used to the bemused expression. It's the same one all the Tech Fair judges have had, because mine is the only board in the cafeteria with graphs in the shape of hearts.

"Libby is a program I developed last summer," I explain. "A matchmaker. And she's never wrong."

"Never?"

"Well, her error rate is 2.9 percent. So almost never."

Mrs. Barkley leans in and studies my narrative, my calculations, and my code. "Impressive. Though I must say, I'm glad we didn't have one of these when I was your age."

"What? Why?"

"Well, I never would have ended up with my husband. He and I are polar opposites." She laughs. "I probably would have gotten stuck with someone like Martin Winsaker. He's the guy my mom wanted me to marry. We actually did go out on a date once, but he was … " She glances around and leans toward me, her voice low. "Handsy. If you know what I mean." She makes a face, and it's all I can do not to laugh.

"Ugh. Who needs handsy boys?"

She shakes her head. "No one." She jots a few notes into her tablet and points her stylus at my poster. "Nice work. Good luck."

I consider her words as she moves on to the next table. *Polar opposites.* They say opposites attract, but Libby doesn't account for that. Nor does she account for the fact that someone who might seem to be a perfect match on paper could turn out to be … handsy. Perhaps there are flaws in the program after all.

"Hey, there!" Lexi saunters down the aisle toward me, interrupting my thoughts. "I love the poster. Way to represent."

I force a smile. "Thanks. Though I'm not sure what exactly I'm representing at this point."

"What?" Lexi points at the highest bar on my graph. "Look at that success rate. You've taken the Boyfriend Whisperer to a new level. You've cracked the code!"

"I guess."

"Hey." Lexi comes around the table to stand next to me. "Are you okay? What's going on?"

I point to the poster. "Sure, Libby has found a lot of perfect matches. But what about all the people who aren't matches but who might still belong together?"

"What do you mean?"

I look away. "Nothing. Never mind."

"Tell me."

I cross my arms. "Darius and I are over."

"Oh, Alicea, I'm sorry. What happened?"

"He wasn't my match. It was a set up. He never even took the stupid survey." I turn to her. "It's just as well, because I was super upset about being matched with him, and he's totally wrong for me, and I never should have gone out with him, and there's no way it was ever going to work with us, and … oh, Lexi, I like him so much."

Lexi wraps me into a hug as I break down in tears. "Hey, hey. It's okay." She waves a couple of judges past my table as I try to pull it together. Finally, she steps back and lifts my chin, forcing me to look at her. "Listen to me. I told you last year that you are beautiful and brilliant and that you have a voice that matters. You said it took you a long time to believe that, but I'm not sure you do believe it, even now."

I wipe at my eyes. "Sometimes I do. Sometimes, not so much. But what does that have to do with whether or not I should date Darius?"

"It has everything to do with it. Because having a voice that matters means actually listening to yourself—to your heart." She points to my poster. "Libby is great, and you should be proud of her. She's made a lot of people really happy, which, let's face it, is the whole point of whispering. But you need to ask yourself: Whose voice matters more? Hers? Or yours?"

Chapter
FIFTY-SEVEN

I stretch my leg along the barre and flex my toes.

"Want some help?" Maggs appears beside me.

"Sure. Thanks."

She gently lifts my leg higher. "How are you doing?"

"Good." I'm not good, but I don't want to bring her down. "So, how did last night go?"

"Oh, it was okay." She looks away.

"Come on, Maggs. Tell me about your date. I'm fine, I swear. And even if I weren't fine, you could tell me. I'm happy for you." I am. She deserves someone like Aiden, someone who adores her and makes her smile the way she has been for the past week. As Lexi said, making people happy is the whole point of whispering.

She shrugs. "Well, there was ice cream—chocolate for me and cookie dough for him. And after that, we stopped in

at a bookstore. He likes poetry. Can you believe that? And …
" Her voice trails off as she lifts my leg another two inches.

"And what?"

"And there may have been some kissing behind one of the shelves."

"Yay! Finally. It only took him three dates."

"I know, but it was … worth the wait."

"That's awesome. Can I ask you something?"

She nods.

"Your secret admirer. Did you want it to be him?"

Maggs's smile widens. "Maybe."

"I'll take that as a yes."

"Aiden is … different from most of the guys I've dated. I feel like he's … I don't know. Right for me somehow."

"Hmm. Imagine that." I haven't told Maggs that Aiden is her match. She'd hate knowing that. I might tell her someday, but not yet.

Ms. DuBois opens the door to her office and calls out to me. "Alicea, may I see you for a moment?"

I give Maggs a quick hug and head over.

Ms. DuBois closes the door behind me and collapses into the chair behind her desk. "I'm exhausted," she says. "We've had more children sign up for our beginner classes than ever before. All four age groups are sold out for the next month."

I smile. "Wow. That's awesome."

"It is. And I have you to thank. And the other dancers, of course. Your First Night performances were very popular with the children and the parents alike. Now everyone wants to be a fairy and a dancer." She leans forward. "And that is what I want to talk to you about."

"Okay."

"The 'Waltz of the Flowers.' Your first performance." She clasps her hands together and beams at me. "I saw it."

"Saw what?"

"It! The passion. The rawness. It was wonderful. Your best dancing ever. It's what I need to see every time."

"Oh. I see." I shake my head. "I don't know if I can do that."

"Why not?"

"Because I don't remember it. The whole dance was a blur to me. My mind was … somewhere else."

"Ah. Then that's the key."

I screw up my lips. Seriously? So all I have to do is have my heart broken before every performance? Come to think of it, at the rate I'm going, maybe that's not so far-fetched.

Ms. DuBois nods at me. "You need to get out of your head. Once you've learned the dance, you need to trust yourself and let go. Let your heart lead the way."

I offer a small smile. She's the second person in two days who's told me to trust my heart. If only it were so simple.

"Ms. DuBois." Monique opens the door and peeks in. "I'm really sorry, but … there's a problem. It's one of the new girls. You'd better come."

Ms. DuBois bolts out toward one of the classrooms, and I follow her.

A crowd of girls has gathered on the far side. "Stand back. Give her some room." One of the instructors is motioning them away. A few of the littlest girls have started to cry.

What's going on?

A woman rushes in, probably the girl's mother, and

kneels down beside her. "Jaycee, can you hear me?"

Jaycee? My blood runs cold. It must be. And she must have had a seizure. I sweep through the crowd until I'm close enough to see. It's her. *Oh my gosh.*

The instructor is speaking to her mom in a low voice. "Her eyes sort of rolled back in her head, and she reached for the barre, but she slipped. I think she hit her head when she went down."

"Oh, no. That could be worse than the seizure itself. We need to call an ambulance."

"Already did." Maggs appears beside me, concern etched on her face. "That's Darius's sister, isn't it?" she whispers to me.

I nod. I don't trust my voice. Poor Jaycee. I feel so helpless. I wish there were something I … Darius. I should call him. He'd want to be here.

As I hit his number, I hear the sound of a siren in the distance. Thank goodness.

He doesn't pick up, which I don't have time to get upset about right now but which is rather upsetting for a few reasons, the most important of which is the fact that there is no way I can leave him a message telling him his sweet little sister had a seizure and will be taken to the hospital. I text him.

```
Alicea: Please call me. It's important.
```

I stare at my phone as a pair of EMT workers rush in with a stretcher. I catch snatches of their conversation: "Unconscious—breathing fine—high heart rate."

Come on, Darius. I know you don't want to hear from me, but this is—

My phone rings.

"Hey." I don't wait for his reply. "I'm sorry to call you like this, but … it's Jaycee. They're taking her to the emergency room."

"What? Is she okay?"

"I think so. I don't know. Your mom is—"

"I'm on my way." He hangs up.

I stare at my phone as Maggs and Brie smother me in a three-way hug.

"Go on," Brie says. "You should be there."

"I don't know. I'll feel weird if—"

"Stop." Maggs points to my head and then to my heart. "Less this. More this."

Chapter
FIFTY-EIGHT

I play game after game of Candy Crush Saga as I sit in the children's unit waiting area. By the time the ambulance arrived at the hospital, Jaycee apparently was conscious and talking, so after some quick tests in the emergency room, they moved her here. Darius has been in her room all evening. I'm not sure when he'll come out, and I'm even less sure I should be here when he does. Still, I'm trying to stick with the whole listen-to-your-heart advice.

I'm figuring out the cannon combination in Valentine Valley when the door to Jaycee's room swings open. My heart pounds, and I close my game.

Darius emerges, his face paler than usual, his eyes dark with worry.

This was a mistake. I turn to leave, but it's too late. He sees me. At first he freezes, but then he comes over. "Hey.

Thanks for calling me. I really appreciate it."

"Of course. How is she?"

He takes a deep breath. "Fine. They were afraid she might have a concussion, but the tests came back negative. She's more embarrassed than anything. It was her first class, and she's afraid if she goes back, the other kids will—"

"No, no, no." I shake my head. "I mean, I guess have no idea what the other kids will do, but I'll beat them up for her if they're not nice."

Darius gives me a side-eye.

"I'm serious."

"Yeah, well, I tried that once." He points to his scar. "It didn't end well."

"You beat up a bunch of ten-year-olds in tutus? And lost?"

That earns a smile. "Not quite," he says. "It was this dude on my basketball team. A real idiot. Jaycee had a seizure at one of our games, and he started making fun of her. I'm not proud of it, but … I snapped."

"It's understandable."

"Well, tell that to my old principal. He didn't understand at all."

"Oh, wow." I feel tears forming, and I'm not sure if it's because I'm worried about Jaycee, or because I feel bad that people can be so horrible, or because I assumed that Darius was a degenerate when in fact he's actually an awesome brother, or because I've screwed things up every step of the way with him. Probably all of the above.

"You're the reason she signed up for dance class, you know."

I blink. "Me? What?"

"Yep. She's talked nonstop about your dancing ever since New Year's. I think you may have surpassed Lexi as her biggest idol."

I laugh. "Doubtful. That's sweet, though. I bet she'll be good at it. She seems like the kind of wonder kid who could be good at both basketball and dance."

Darius smiles. "She's a wonder kid, all right."

We stand for a moment in silence, and then, because I don't know what else to say, I give him a hug. "I guess I should go. I'm glad she's okay." I turn to leave, but when I reach the door, I stop and turn back. "Darius, can we talk?"

"Of course."

"I mean, I don't want to interfere with … " I wave toward Jaycee's room.

"It's fine. My mom's in there with her. They're processing the paperwork for her discharge." He glances around the waiting room and nods toward the door. "Come on. I need to get some air."

We head outside and wander over to my car. We climb in, and I pump up the heat. "So." I take a deep breath. "I owe you an apology. I've been a complete and total idiot."

He says nothing as he fiddles with the latch on my glove compartment. I take his silence as permission to continue.

"The thing is, I'm a paint-by-numbers kind of person. I like it when one equals red, and two equals blue, and three equals yellow, but you … " I shake my head. "You don't have a number. You're like this huge part of the picture with no number attached, and I don't know what to do with you."

"Why do you have to do anything?" He turns and meets

my gaze. "I don't want to have a number, Alicea. I don't want to fit some formula, because that's not real. You like order and algorithms? That's cool. I love that about you. But it doesn't work with people. Because people are messy."

I consider this. What was it my mom said that night in her class? Sometimes art is about appreciating the imperfect. I reach out and touch his scar, an imperfection he earned protecting his sister. "You're right," I say. "I'm sorry. I've been so hung up on finding my perfect match that I've refused to appreciate the amazingly imperfect one right in front of me."

He laughs. "Thanks. I think?"

I lean back against my door. "I wish we could start over. No formulas. Just you and me and all our messy imperfections."

His eyebrows shoot up. "You? Have imperfections?"

"Ha, ha. I'm pretty sure those have been on full display lately." I close my eyes. "I am so stupid."

"No, you're not. You're like the near-perfect flower you made. Reaching. And I am rooting for you."

"Thanks. That's still a terrible pun, you know."

"Come on. You sure it isn't *growing* on you?"

I groan. "Please stop."

"Or what? You'll ... *leave?*"

I narrow my eyes at him. "Maybe. Now that you've *planted the seed.*"

"Woah." He smiles appreciatively and makes an explosion with his fist, his fingers pointed upward. "*BLOOM!*"

I can't help but laugh. "You are such a goof."

"That's me. A numberless goof."

I'm dying to reach up and touch his curls, but I resist. Instead, I clasp my hands in my lap. "Maybe you're right.

Maybe numbers are overrated."

He leans toward me, his eyes studying mine. "Are you serious about wanting to start over?"

I nod. "Can we?"

He takes my hand in his. "You're sure? Even though we're an imperfect match?"

"I'm sure."

He hesitates. "You say that now, but what if—"

"Darius." I wrap my pinkie around his. "I promise. I'm serious. I want to start over. You and me—imperfect together."

"In that case … " He leans forward and kisses me—a long, soft, sweet kiss that is as close to perfect as a kiss can get.

As we pull away, his eyes focus on something outside the window. "Hey. Would you look at that?"

I turn, but I don't see anything. "Look at what?"

He smiles. "The way the parking lot light was glowing behind your head. It looked a little bit like a halo."

THE END

Acknowledgements

As always, while this book may have my name on the cover, it represents the efforts and support of so many. I am thankful to each of you, with special thanks to:

Georgia McBride, Laura Whitaker, and everyone at Swoon Romance for seeing the possibilities in this book and helping me to get it there; Andrea Somberg for her awesome agenting; and Danielle Doolittle for once again wielding her cover magic.

My writing friends, both IRL and virtual, and especially to Ellen Braaf, Kathy Chappell, and the many folks of SCBWI Mid-Atlantic.

My church family, and especially the SUMC LifeSigns youth.

My family-family—Joe, Eris, and Sarah; Bea and Ted Acorn; Deb, Karen, and Ted; and my extended family, who all have been so super supportive of my books.

My readers—I owe you all so many heart emojis!

And God, in whom all things are possible.

Linda Acorn Budzinski

Linda Budzinski is the author of four young adult novels: *The Boyfriend Whisperer 2.0, The Boyfriend Whisperer, Em & Em*, and *The Funeral Singer*. She lives in Northern Virginia with her husband, Joe, and their crazy pup JoJo. She's a sucker for romance and reality TV, and of course, matchmaking, so she's known to turn off her phone's ringer when watching *The Bachelor*. Her favorite flower is the daisy, her favorite food is chocolate, and her favorite song is "Amazing Grace." When she's not writing, she works in non-profit communications and outreach.

OTHER SWOON ROMANCE TITLES YOU MIGHT LIKE

THE BOYFRIEND WHISPERER
EM & EM
THE FUNERAL SINGER

Find more books like this at http://www.myswoonromance.com

Connect with Swoon Romance online:
Facebook: https://www.Facebook.com/swoonromance
Instagram: http://www.instagram.com/swoonromance
Twitter: https://twitter.com/SwoonRomance
Tumblr: http://swoonromance.tumblr.com/
Georgia McBride Media Group: www.georgiamcbride.com

THE *boyfriend* WHISPERER

LOVE IS BUT A WHISPER AWAY

LINDA BUDZINSKI

THE
Funeral Singer
LINDA BUDZINSKI

CPSIA information can be obtained
at www.ICGtesting.com
Printed in the USA
BVHW032334240219
541064BV00001B/126/P